Christine Pullein-Thompson has been involved with horses all her life—she opened a riding school with her sisters when she was fourteen. She started writing at fifteen and published her first book with her sisters Diana and Josephine. Christine has written more than 90 books which have been translated into nine languages. She is best known for her pony books but has also written the highly successful Jessie series about a dog and general fiction stories for younger readers.

Christine has four children and lives with her husband Julian Popescu in a moated Parsonage in Suffolk with two horses, a dog and a cat.

D1513987

Other Pony Books by Christine Pullein-Thompson

Published by *Cavalier Paperbacks*

Stolen Ponies
I Rode A Winner
The Lost Pony
For Want of A Saddle

A PONY IN DISTRESS

Christine Pullein-Thompson

**CAVALIER
PAPERBACKS**

© Christine Pullein-Thompson 1994

Published by Cavalier Paperbacks 1994
PO Box 1821, Warminster, Wilts BA12 0YD

Cover Design by Michelle Bellfield
Cover Photograph by Alistair Fyfe
Courtesy of The Infantry Saddle Club, Warminster

ISBN 1–899470–00–X

Typeset in New Century Schoolbook and Ottawa
by Ann Buchan (Typesetters), Shepperton
Printed and bound by
Cox and Wyman, Reading, Berkshire

CONTENTS

1. I'm Calling Him Snowman   7

2. Sarah   15

3. A Christmas To Remember   24

4. The Ears of A Mule   37

5. Go, Find Rob   46

6. A Long Night   58

7. The Siege   74

8. I Don't Want Other Ponies   83

9. Dressage   92

10. The Show   101

11. Waiting   113

12. No More Hate   123

Chapter One

I'M CALLING HIM SNOWMAN

Rob filled the pockets of his anorak with carrots.

"Where are you taking those?" asked his mother.

"Where do you think?"

"To the old pony tethered up the lane," she replied.

Snow was beginning to fall, snow on snow. Rob found his boots. One of his legs was shorter than the other; he was not crippled, just a little disabled. That's the way he saw it, and he tried not to think about it. I have a limp so what? he asked himself when someone remarked on his disability. In spite of that every comment hurt. Rob was nearly eleven with a mop of dark hair, brown eyes and a nose which turned up at the end. Small for his age, he lived in isolated Yew Tree Farm with his parents, two cats and an ancient spaniel. He should have been lonely there, but he wasn't—illness, plus two operations had given him an inner strength and he was grateful for what he had—the ability to walk and talk, for it had not always been like that.

Now his mother said, "Well don't be long love, soon it will be dark."

He had been feeding the pony every evening after school for weeks. Now school had broken up for Christmas and he had almost forgotten. As Rob stepped outside, a flurry of snow swept across the farmyard; then he could see his father driving across the fields in a tractor, his cap on his head. He looked indestructible, but Rob knew he wasn't, because he had seen him in tears a few weeks ago when the bank manager had telephoned to say that his bank account was overdrawn by thousands of pounds. His mother had started to go out to work after that, and they had survived; but they all knew it was going to be a hard winter—the hardest ever.

The old grey pony whinnied when he saw Rob. Icicles hung from his long, unkempt mane; he was coated with snow. He had stood there all day long tied by a chain to an iron stake driven into the hard ground, a stake which had not been moved for two days.

Rob took the carrots from his pocket and gave them to the pony. Nothing seemed to be moving and the snow muffled all sound. Then Rob couldn't decide what to do and stood looking for help, for someone to arrive and care for the pony because he could see now that he was ill, perhaps even dying. But no-one came, only a small spiteful wind arrived from no-where and blew the snow into his eyes. Afterwards Rob couldn't say how long he had stood there. It seemed a long time, but probably it was no more than ten minutes. And all the while he was hoping that the pony's owner would appear in his van and take the pony into the rotten ramshackle stable and fetch him an armful of the musty hay which lay under a tarpaulin nearby. He had done it every evening until now. Why not tonight? wondered Rob shivering.

At last, Rob did what he had been wanting to do for some time. He unclipped the chain from the pony's headcollar and said, "You're coming home. You're going to be inside. You're not staying here a moment longer." And now they were both shivering with cold. For a moment the pony could not move; he seemed frozen to the spot where he had waited for so long for the arrival of the man who everyone knew as Bill.

Rob patted his neck. "Come on, or we'll both die of cold if we hang about," he said. Slowly they moved towards the farmhouse, which crouched low in the valley. "You're going to be all right," Rob told the pony as he walked. "You're not going to be cold any more."

Rob's mother was outside waiting for him. "Thank goodness," she cried. "I thought you were never coming back. But what are you doing with the pony?"

"I've brought him home. There's no-one in the caravan. He was freezing to death Mum," Rob called. "I couldn't leave him there."

"You look cold yourself," she said snapping on lights. "Bring him over here. We'll put him in the calf shed, just for tonight. He'll have to go back in the morning, you know that, don't you? First thing. Your Dad can't take him on, we have too many problems already."

Rob didn't answer. He just went on talking to the pony, saying, "It's all right, you'll be all right here. You won't be cold any more."

"Hasn't he got a name?" asked Rob's mother fetching a bale of straw and spreading it across the calf shed's floor.

"No, he's not called anything. Bill just calls him 'the pony'. I really think Bill should be prosecuted, I really do Mum. Another night out and he would have been dead."

The pony looked round the stable and saw straw and soon hay and a bucket of water, which all seemed to appear by magic. The water was clean, the hay smelt sweet, and the straw was thick and welcoming, and he gave a great sigh of happiness. Then the icicles on his mane started to melt and his eyes were like dark velvet in his haggard old face. He lay down in the straw with another sigh and suddenly Rob was afraid he would never get up again. He saw the old pony dying and blamed himself, even though he was doing the only decent thing in the circumstances—bringing him home.

"I'll get him a hot mash with black treacle in it. Stay with him Rob," his mother said, her voice suddenly thick with distress. And that's Mum all over thought Rob fondly. For she hated anything dying; when the cattle went to market she couldn't speak for days. Dad had often said that she should never have married a farmer. She was too soft, he said.

Rob knelt in the straw by the pony and fed him hay; then he fetched a sack, the old hemp kind, and put it over his quarters. "You're going to be all right, I promise," he said, before his father's figure stood in the doorway blocking out the snow which was still falling outside.

"What have we here? Not the old pony?" he asked.

"He was dying. Bill isn't there, the caravan's emp-

10

ty. I looked. I couldn't leave him Dad, not there all alone in the snow," Rob replied.

"No of course you couldn't, but I had better leave a note to tell Bill his pony's here, hadn't I?" his father asked. " I'll go now. We don't want the police called out, not in this weather."

Rob loved his father, but not as much as he loved his mother, who reappeared now with a warm mash, with carrots in it, in one hand, and a blanket in the other. They pulled the pony up and put on the blanket, tying it around his middle with binder twine. He was steaming already, and his eyes looked brighter as he tucked into the mash.

"He's going to be all right," Rob's mother said. "But I wish he had a name and a kind owner. We don't need any more animals to look after, Rob."

"I'm calling him Snowman, because he looked like one when I found him," Rob said. "And I want him to stay here for ever."

"We can't afford a pony, and you can't ride. Why I doubt whether you could even mount with your poor leg," his mother replied walking ahead towards the house.

"You'd be surprised," Rob muttered. "I want to keep him. All right?" he shouted. "I want something of my own, all right?"

His mother ignored him and soon they sat down to tea in the old fashioned kitchen. His father returned home and taking off his hat and coat, said, "Not a sign of the old blighter. How can he keep a pony like that?"

"It's diabolical," replied Rob's mother. "He'll have

to be prosecuted. Perhaps we should get an inspector out tomorrow."

"If anyone can get anywhere. The snow is more than a metre deep in places," replied Rob's father tucking into baked beans on toast.

Then Bill won't be able to return from wherever he is. Perhaps he's dead. I hope he is, thought Rob viciously. I hope he's freezing to death somewhere. He deserves it.

Twice that evening Rob went out to look at Snowman, the second time the snow was almost over his boots. Both times Snowman whinnied when he saw him coming. Rob patted him. He was no beauty; his ears were too long for his lean grey face, his neck too thin, his hocks too large, his knees too boney. There were deep lines on his haunches and his hoofs were ragged with one still shod, the others shoeless. He rubbed his head up and down against Rob's coat as though trying to say 'thank you'. The calf shed was perfect for him, neither too big nor too small, and it smelt lovely, of steaming pony and well made hay.

"Tomorrow I'll brush you," Rob said. "I'll remove the tangles from your mane, and the matts from beneath your belly. I won't forget."

"Don't get too fond of the pony," said Mum later, as Rob prepared for bed. "Remember he isn't yours. All right love, just remember."

"He's not 'the pony', he's Snowman, and I am remembering," Rob answered clambering into bed. "And I would like to kill old Bill. I mean it Mum, I really do."

"You mustn't say that," replied his mother.

"But I can think it. No-one can stop me thinking what I like," replied Rob. "And just now I'm thinking that I'd like Bill dead in a snow drift, or killed in a car crash, because he doesn't deserve to live—Snowman's like a toast rack, or haven't you noticed? He has been for weeks. He's been standing out there all day without a scrap of shelter, all weathers. It's disgusting," Rob finished.

"Well he'll be all right tonight anyway," replied Rob's mother switching off the light.

"Bill should go to prison for years and years," Rob said.

"Don't work yourself up Rob or you won't sleep," replied his mother closing the door as she went out.

"He should be hung," Rob shouted after her.

"Now you're being silly," she answered going downstairs.

It wasn't dark because of the snow. Outside everything was quiet and very still. It was three days to Christmas. Rob's mother had brought in holly from the high hedge in the top meadow. His father had brought a tree from the spinney, which ran between their property and the next. Rob lay in bed thinking about Christmas. If Snowman was still with them on Christmas Day he would make him a special breakfast full of chopped carrot and apple, and he would groom him till he was clean and sleek. If Bill took him back to his place Rob would give him his breakfast just the same. But it would be very sad and Christmas would be spoilt for all of them. Rob wished now that he had talked to Bill more. He could have asked him why he kept a pony and where the pony had come from. But in all the times Rob had been visiting Snowman there, they had never once held a proper conversation. But then Bill didn't really talk to anyone. He kept himself to himself. He didn't mix and was an uncouth man who smelt because he never had a bath. Bill lived alone in the caravan; only the patch of land where Snowman had been tethered was his. Rob knew that if you asked Bill anything, he rarely answered, just went about his business fetching in wood, or separating the old iron he had collected in his van, without a word. People said that once upon a time he had been a scrap dealer with a daughter. But no-one knew anything for certain, only that Bill sat in the pub, which was called the Gooseberry Bush, every evening drinking beer in a corner.

He had his own beer tankard there and his own bar stool. People said he never talked to anyone. So why did he keep Snowman? Rob wondered, his mind going round and round in circles—why? There had to be an answer. But before Rob found it he was overcome by sleep.

Chapter Two

SARAH

When Rob went to see Snowman the next morning, his father had already fed him, and there was clean water in the bucket in the corner of the calf shed. The pony looked more cheerful. The blanket had slipped over one side. Rob took it off and hung it over the door. He had no dandy brush to groom with, but his mother found him an unused scrubbing brush which he used instead. Soon he found itchy patches under Snowman's mane and he called to his father, "Come and look Dad. I think he's got lice."

"Yes, you're right Rob. I'll find you some powder. But you know he'll have to go back eventually, make no mistake about that. I can't afford to keep someone else's pony, not as things are in farming at present. I'm sorry son, but there it is," his father said.

"I know that," Rob replied. "So you don't have to keep telling me."

He was working on Snowman's tail when his father returned with a large carton of Coopers louse powder. "Shake it all over him, especially behind his ears and along his rump. He looks terrible doesn't he? I'm ashamed to have him on my farm," his father said.

"You can feel between his ribs; there's nothing there," Rob replied. His father nodded and went back to his pigs. The snow was melting and the sun was up. There were only two days left until Christmas now but it felt like summer.

Rob talked to the pony as he worked, but all the time he was listening for someone to come and take him away. If that happened he knew that Christmas would be ruined, because he would not care about it any more; the decorations would mock him and the food would stick in his throat; for all the time he would be seeing Snowman going back to the waste patch and Bill.

Soon Rob was covered in the fine white louse powder and Snowman had become tired of being deloused and was standing at the back of the shed, which fitted so perfectly that it might have been made specially.

Rob went outside bolting the door after him and saw a girl wheeling a white bike into the yard. She was wearing riding clothes and suddenly his heart stopped beating and began pounding with fear. She was older than him with fair hair and a large generous mouth and hazel eyes. "I'm looking for a grey pony," she said. "A friend of yours told me he was here." Rob stared at her. "I haven't got a friend," he snapped.

"His name is Mark, and you led the pony past his house yesterday," she explained, leaning her bike against the yard wall.

"Oh him. I'll have to go and wash. I'll be back in a minute." Rob hurried to the house, his heart racing, and washed his hands at the sink and went out again into the unexpected sunshine.

"You're hurt. What happened? You're limping," the girl said.

"Nothing. Nothing at all."

She was looking at him critically now, noticing his shortened leg, taking it all in. "I suppose it's permanent. I'm sorry I didn't mean to be inquisitive," she explained, her face suddenly red with embarrassment.

"It doesn't matter," Rob replied. "I never think about it."

"He looks better doesn't he, quite different already," said the girl looking at Snowman.

"You should be prosecuted, or your Dad should. He was dying yesterday. He could hardly move, he was frozen stiff." Rob's voice wasn't his own now. He knew he was sounding emotional instead of firm and condemning. "What do you want to do anyway? Take him back to his miserable existence?" And now without wanting to, he was shouting.

"What's your name?" the girl was smiling at him now and he hated her.

"Robert Bartrum, Rob to my friends."

"I'm Sarah. And he's not my pony, and that terrible old man is not my Dad and, if he was, I think I would kill myself," she continued laughing. "Oh Rob, do I look like the sort of person who would abandon a pony or leave it tethered outside in the cold? I've been worried stiff about him. I was going to ring the police, or my horsy aunt. Then I came to look at him one more time and he wasn't there. I'm just so glad he's here. I really am. I'm over the moon about it Rob. Are you going to keep him for ever? Have you come to some arrangement?"

Rob wished she wouldn't ask so many questions. 'Nosey', his mother would have called her. "I don't know what's going to happen. Dad had left a note in that horrible man's caravan saying his pony is here. I hate him, I really do. He should be locked up. How could be behave like that?" Rob finished.

"He's not back. I looked on the way. I'd better go now. I'll give you my telephone number so if you need reinforcements, give me a ring. I'm willing to stand up in Court and say what I think, and we must take him to Court for cruelty, mustn't we? I'll get my aunt to come and look at the pony, she'll write a report. She's an expert. Okay?" She didn't give him time to reply but scribbled a number on a piece of paper and gave it to him.

"Is she a vet?" Rob asked taking the bit of paper.

"Yes she is, and she won't charge you anything. I'll twist her arm, okay? You don't mind do you? I was going to ring her anyway."

Rob shook his head. Sarah was mounting her bike now. "What do you call him?" she asked. "Has he a name?"

"Yes, 'the pony', but I call him Snowman," Rob replied.

"Most suitable," Sarah called laughing as she left the yard.

Rob took the piece of paper indoors and showed it to his mother.

"Goodness me," she said. "I hope you were polite—she's the Rector's daughter, a lovely girl people say."

Rob read what was on the piece of paper. Sarah

Riley, The Rectory, followed by a telephone number.

"She seemed all right, quite nice I suppose," he said. "She says she'll help if I need her and she's sending her aunt to look at Snowman. She's a vet, but I don't think we'll have to pay, so Dad can't grumble can he?"

"Fair enough", his mother answered and made him sit down and eat breakfast. Presently his Dad appeared saying, "Who was that young lady then?" Rob didn't answer because he was remembering the feeling of fear which had gripped him when Sarah appeared, and he was wondering whether it would ever go away. And he couldn't explain even to himself, why he wanted the old pony so much, or why the pony's happiness now seemed more important than anything else. He ate his breakfast but he didn't taste it, because all the time he was imagining Bill driving into the yard in his rusty old van, getting out, demanding, "Where is he? Give him back to me. He isn't yours." And the very thought of it made Rob want to weep.

His mother had strung up the holly across the beams in the old kitchen. Already there was a pile of presents under the Christmas tree in the sitting room, and a heap of cards on the table. But Rob didn't care too much about Christmas this year, because now there was only one thing he wanted, and that was to keep Snowman. More than anything else he wanted something of his own to care about, to manage and to love. And he knew that if the old grey pony went back to Bill he would never get over it, neither of them would.

"I was going into town, but I won't if a vet's coming," Rob's mother said as she washed and he dried the breakfast things. "Did you like Sarah?"

"I don't know," replied Rob remembering her remark about his limp.

Later that day, Sarah's aunt appeared. She did not resemble the vets who usually visited the farm. She drove a Saab for one thing, and she looked well off, the sort of person who would sit on committees.

"I'm Ann Casting" she said and shook Mrs Bartrum's hand and said to Rob, "What's the matter with your leg then?" In that way she was like Sarah he thought—tactless.

"It's a long story. He was born with it," Mrs Bartrum said, sounding tired.

"Has he seen the best people," asked Ann Casting, alluding to Doctors, Rob supposed.

"Yes, he's had several operations," replied Rob's mother as though that settled the matter.

Having disposed of that problem, Ann Casting went to look at Snowman. Rob found he was trembling as she felt the pony all over, then fetched a stethoscope from her car and listened to his chest. After that she straightened her back and looked at Rob's mother. "He's got pneumonia; he's got no flesh on him, he's riddled with worms, he's lousy. He's really sick and he's been sick for some time," she continued, glancing at Rob who felt like groaning with despair.

"He hasn't been coughing and he is eating," Rob's mother replied, not daring to look at Rob because they both knew what was coming next.

"Poor old fellow," said Sarah's aunt. "It's such a shame. He must have been a smashing pony in his day. Do you know anything about his past?" Rob shook his head miserably.

"Well I don't think he's worth saving; it wouldn't be fair on him," said Ann Casting, looking outside at the melting snow. "It's better to let him go. I'll fix everything up for you."

"It's all right. My husband can do that," said Rob's mother.

"If he wasn't so old it would be different," Ann Casting continued, looking at Snowman's teeth. "He's fifteen at least, and he's had a hard time of it poor old fellow and he may end up with a broken wind, even if we do get him well again."

"Is it the cost you're thinking of?" asked Rob's mother patting the pony's thin grey neck.

"Yes, and I think it's better for him; he's still got a long winter ahead, and he may never recover, he may have red worm, the worm may have perforated his intestines. He's very sick Mrs Bartrum. He's been sick a long time." Rob started to cry quietly. "To put it simply, it could cost a lot to get him right, and at the end of the day he may still be unrideable," she finished. "Think it over. Give me a ring tonight if you need any more help. But that's my advice."

"I have deloused him, and we could worm him, we could give it a try couldn't we?" Rob asked desperately. "And if he was a person he wouldn't be put down would he? He would be sent to hospital." As he spoke Rob's voice rose in hopeless anger. "If he were a person, he would be nursed back to health wouldn't he?" he finished.

"Life is full of ifs, and he isn't a person," replied Sarah's aunt, getting into her car. "There's a hell of a difference between a person and an old pony, Rob. You should know that, being a farmer's son. Wake up. We must be practical. Ask your parents to buy you a younger animal; though with your leg, it might be better if you had lessons with Riding for the Disabled," she said.

"I hate her, I hate her, and I hate Bill. I think I'm beginning to hate all humans," Rob cried wiping his eyes as she drove away.

"We're going to save Snowman, Rob. I've made up my mind. We'll get the farm vet to look at him. So cheer up, love. Come on, it will be a challenge," his mother said. And now Rob was glad that his father wasn't there to agree with Sarah's aunt, to say, 'Okay I'll see to it, we can't keep an old pony here eating his head off, if he's never going to get any better. I'll ring the abattoir. I know what to do.' But his mother was different. She had released all the hens from their sickening battery cages and put them in ark houses on the stubble. She loved animals. And Rob was like his mother. He wanted the animals to roam free, to enjoy their often short lives. Then he thought, but how can we put Snowman down when he isn't ours? And what can we do if Bill arrives and claims him back and then starts tethering him all over again whatever the weather? And he thought, perhaps Sarah's aunt is right, perhaps it's better for him to be destroyed rather than return to being tethered, and now it seemed the saddest moment of his life. His mother put her arms around his shoulders. "We're going to get him well again, I promise," she said. "It may take time, but we'll do it."

"And if Bill returns?" asked Rob.

"We'll face that when it happens. One thing at a time. We can always call on that woman to give evidence against him. And we can get Bill taken to Court for cruelty to animals," his mother answered, and Rob knew now that she too disliked Sarah's aunt, by the words 'that woman'. "And don't worry about your leg, it's all right, there's worse things than a gammy leg, far worse, it's just a hiccup really," she added.

Then Rob went into the kitchen and chopped apples and carrots and took them out to Snowman, who nickered when he saw Rob coming, his old grey head looking over the calf shed door which they were already calling 'Snowman's Stable'.

Rob's father appeared and leaning on the door asked, "Well, what did the dragon say?"

"Not a lot," replied Rob.

"Wanted to put him down I suppose?"

Rob nodded.

"Well we won't do that. We'll give him a chance, keep him going till the spring grass comes through again, let him have a good summer. Then we'll think again."

"And if Bill turns up?" asked Rob surprised.

"I'll deal with him. Don't you worry. He won't come here twice," his father said. "I'll tell him a thing or two."

Chapter Three

A CHRISTMAS TO REMEMBER

The next day the farm vet called. He was middle-aged in old clothes and muddy boots. He was called Jim Hubbard. "You want to save him, do you?" he asked entering Snowman's stable.

Rob nodded. Jim Hubbard felt Snowman all over, listened to his chest, looked into his eyes, listened to his heart, picked up each leg in turn, and all the time he talked to Snowman, saying things like, "Easy there. Good pony. You've had a bad time, poor old chap." He took his temperature and looked inside his mouth.

After a time he stood back and looked at Snowman. Rob found that he was trembling again. "Well it's touch and go, but if you really want to save him, we'll give it a go. His heart's quite strong and that's a good point, but we can't be sure if he's all right inside, not unless you want to send him to have a scan, and that won't be cheap," he said.

"We'll leave that for now, just the basics Jim,"replied Mr Bartrum.

"Antibiotics first then." Jim moved quickly and quietly. He slipped a needle into Snowman's neck. Then handed Mr Bartrum a worm syringe and Rob medicine to be mixed with feeds. "Is he the old pony which was tethered?" he asked.

"That's right." Rob was trying to smile, to be grateful.

"I kept meaning to do something about him. His owner should have been prosecuted long ago," Jim Hubbard said.

"That's what people keep saying. But they didn't do anything," replied Rob.

"That's life. I'll drop you in a rug later today, you need a proper one with a surcingle. I've got one at home going spare. And I'll do his teeth after Christmas," said Jim Hubbard smiling at Rob, thinking that he was more like his mother than his father, and how unlucky he was to be cursed with a limp.

"Ring me tomorrow and let me know how he is. Now let's look at the cow with mastitis," he said.

"Well, where there's life there's hope," said Rob's mother who had been watching the proceedings. "And vets are usually pessimistic Rob, so I think Snowman will recover. I do really."

It was Christmas Eve now. Rob should have been excited but he wasn't. His mother went indoors to make mince-pies while Rob fussed over Snowman, shaking up his hay, refilling his water bucket, straightening his mane.

A little later Sarah appeared in the yard. "You've still got him then?" she asked leaning over the door, looking at Rob working on Snowman's tail. "What did my aunt say?"

"Not a lot."

"Do you know how to look after a pony?"

"Dad does. Dad's looked after animals all his life," Rob answered.

"Well don't give him calf cubes, or pig food, they're full of hormones and sedatives, things like that. I thought my aunt would say he was to be put down. I don't suppose he'll ever recover completely anyway," she said.

"She did, but we aren't paying any attention." (Rob enjoyed saying that.)

"So you've had another vet?"

Rob nodded. "We're going to try and save him."

"And if Bill comes back and demands his return?" asked Sarah.

"Dad will deal with him."

"But he could be tethered all over again," Sarah said.

"We won't let it happen. There's a new act anyway. It's called The Cruel Tethering Act." Rob didn't know how he knew that, somebody must have told him about it, but who and when he could not recall.

"Well, it's your affair, but my aunt won't be pleased. She's very well known. I ride her ponies for her. She's married to Lord Casting, she's really an Hon."

Rob walked out of Snowman's stable and bolted the door. "Do you want some coffee? If so come inside, there's some mince-pies just out of the oven," he said.

"Dad is in a fuss over tomorrow. He always is. Christmas is very important if you're a Rector," Sarah said following him inside.

Rob disliked her following him, imagining she was

26

observing his limp, pitying him. Because of that he walked faster and hobbled more.

Mostly she talked to his mother after that, sitting at the large cluttered table stuffing mince-pies, talking about life in the Rectory, about the long cold passages and the boiler which kept going out. She made Mrs Bartrum laugh and for once Sarah wasn't tactless, praising the mince-pies, admiring the Dutch dresser, doing her best to please, sounding older than her years. Rob's mother lapped it all up, instantly wishing that she had such a daughter herself. Presently Rob's father came inside and she charmed him too. "What a wonderful girl," they said after she had gone and Rob who had remained silent throughout was jealous.

He went outside and talked to Snowman who looked fatter already, but was still a skeleton. Pippa, the elderly spaniel turned out of the kitchen because her paws were dirty, soon joined them and she and Snowman made friends by sniffing noses, and all the while Christmas Day was growing nearer and still Rob was not excited.

When he returned inside, his mother said, "Sarah left you this," and handed him an envelope. Inside was a card, on which horses galloped into a vivid sunset. Inside she had written, To Rob, Love Sarah.

"How sweet of her," Rob's mother said reading it over his shoulder. "She really is a lovely girl."

Later that day Mr Bartrum went to the Gooseberry Tree for a drink and returned with news. "Bill's in custody, so we won't be seeing him this Christmas," he said.

27

"In prison you mean, awaiting trial? Is that it?" Rob's mother asked and Rob's father nodded, adding, "He's been stealing bits off cars. It's not the first time. He'll probably get six months."

And straightaway Rob was counting the months on his fingers, working out that Bill would be let out in June and by then Snowman would be well or dead.

"The police have been all over his caravan." His father was still talking, but Rob wasn't listening any more; he was far away imagining a sunny day and himself riding a recovered Snowman. He was riding alongside Sarah, feeling her equal, his limp forgotten.

Before it was dark, Rob led Snowman up the lane a little way. The pony didn't want to leave the stable and hurried home. As Rob reached the yard, Jim Hubbard appeared with a jute night rug under his arm. He helped Rob put it on saying, "He looks a little better. We had better keep our fingers crossed. Have a good Christmas. Don't let him spoil it for you all; whatever happens, he will have had a good end." He waved before he left and called 'Happy Christmas'.

Rob thought, he thinks he's going to die, and twice that night he got up and putting on his dressing gown and boots, went outside to look at Snowman. Both times the old pony was lying down, looking warm and content in his rug, still breathing, though the second time his breathing seemed too fast which made Rob feel sick with anxiety.

His mother appeared saying, "Is he all right? Happy Christmas," and the sky was full of stars and nearly all the snow had gone.

"I had to look at him," Rob said.

"I know. I couldn't sleep either. Later we'll go to church and you can pray for him," his mother replied, leading the way back indoors.

"Can you pray for horses? Is God interested? Is it allowed?"

"I don't see why not. You can pray for anything, Rob. God isn't a politician," she said and laughed.

"I'll go then." Rob had only been to church once and then he had lost his way in the prayer book.

"Go back to bed. I think Father Christmas has been," his mother said. and when he went upstairs again he found a stocking at the foot of his bed full of wonderful things. And now the cocks were crowing outside, and the stars were fading in the night sky. Snowman's survived another night, he's going to be all right, Rob thought, and his heart sang.

Pippa scratched on the door and he let her in and she sat on his bed sharing the chocolate which had been in his stocking. And everything was suddenly hopeful because it was Christmas and unexpectedly it held its usual magic, which was so mystical and wonderful that it defied words.

Later that day they opened their presents and went to church. Sarah was there looking different in a dress and coat. She talked to them afterwards asking about Snowman, saying that he was a lucky pony to be with them. Rob had prayed for Snowman to get better soon, and was now filled with hope. When he felt like this he forgot his limp. He had looked at Sarah's father during the sermon and seen a tall, angular man, dressed in white and red because it was Christmas. The church was almost full and his parents seemed to know almost everyone there. And now it seemed as if nothing could spoil the day. Snowman had been with them for nearly four days, and time should be on their side, he thought, watching his mother talking to an enormous woman with a wiry little husband.

"See you," said Sarah and disappeared towards the Rectory.

"Come on you two, time for our Christmas dinner," called Rob's father who liked food, meat most of all.

They piled into the car. The sun was shining, the grass still tinselled with the night's frost.

"I'm glad we came. We should do it more often," Rob's mother said. "Did you pray for Snowman, Rob?"

"Yes." He was embarrassed because he felt that prayers should be secret, something private between yourself and God.

"Sarah is a lovely girl," his mother continued. "And she could be a help to you, Rob."

When the car was parked, Rob went straight to see Snowman. His head was not hanging over the door which seemed strange. Another minute and Rob was staring at him lying in the straw, his head turned towards his flank, groaning. Then Rob was shouting, "Snowman's ill. Quick. He's in agony." And Christmas and his prayers were forgotten and all which mattered was Snowman.

His parents appeared immediately. "It's colic," his father said. "Get him up and don't let him roll. Where's his halter?"

Another minute and Snowman was standing outside, his neck damp with sweat, his sides heaving.

"We'd better call Jim out," Mrs Bartrum said.

"What on Christmas Day? It will cost a fortune," Rob's father retorted.

"And spoil his Christmas too," his mother added, but went towards the house regardless, determined to save Snowman whatever the cost.

"He's trying to roll again, help me someone—please," shouted Rob. Tugging on the headcollar rope, feeling frantic and sick at the same time, Rob was thinking, if I had not gone to church this might never have happened, blaming himself as he so often did for anything which went wrong.

"Don't panic, it's just a touch of colic," his father said in his slow calm voice, taking the rope, saying to Snowman, "Come on. Get up old fella. Come on, that's better," as Snowman heaved himself up and stood trembling.

"He's soaked in sweat. He must be in agony to sweat like that, Rob cried.

"Jim's on his way," announced his mother minutes later.

"What did he say?" Rob asked.

"Not a lot. Things always happen at Christmas, it's not the first time is it, Charlie?" she asked Rob's father who was walking Snowman backwards and forwards across the yard, still wearing his best suit, which was now flecked with grey hairs.

"I wish we had never gone to church. I wish I had stayed here," Rob cried, and wondered why he had bothered to pray for Snowman to get better, when the result was so devastating.

31

"You can't be with him all the time. You'll be sleeping with him next," his mother said. "Be reasonable, love."

A watery winter sun shone down on them. Snowman was still sweating. He looked as though he wasn't really with them, and wouldn't even eat a carrot. I'm too old to cry, thought Rob, but cried just the same, looking away from his parents, not wanting them to see his tears.

His mother brought them mugs of coffee. She had taken the turkey out of the oven, turned off the heat under the Christmas pudding. It didn't seem like Christmas to her now, more like a usual day.

A mile away Sarah was telling her aunt about Snowman, who said, "Well it's their funeral," when Sarah paused for breath. "But it will be worse for them if he dies a natural death."

"What's the matter with the boy's leg? Is it inherited or was he hurt?"

"I think he was born like that. A lady in the village told Dad that he was a walking miracle. He's cute," she added. "And he's not stupid either."

Jim arrived. "It's colic or worse," he announced after glancing at Snowman. "Get him inside."

"What do you mean? What's worse?" Rob asked in a scared voice.

"Twisted gut, perforated lung, collapse of the kidneys; though I don't think it's that," Jim replied. "He was pretty sick when you found him, and thin, which could have been caused by underfeeding, or something worse, sometimes it's difficult to tell without a scan."

"We'll have a scan then," replied Rob's mother firmly, while his father raised his eyes to heaven thinking of the cost.

"They won't be giving scans on Christmas Day, not for an old pony like this one. Maybe if he was a famous race horse it would be different. I'll sedate him, then give him an enema and we'll take it from there," Jim said and Rob noticed that he was wearing a brand new tie, probably a Christmas present he thought.

"I'm sorry we've spoilt your Christmas," Rob's mother said.

"It's what we're here for," replied Jim without smiling.

And now standing in church, singing THE FIRST NOEL, suddenly seemed a different world to Rob.

They stood about waiting for Snowman to grow drowsy. Jim kept looking at his watch. Rob thought, if Snowman dies Sarah's aunt will say, "I told you so."

The enema didn't take long. "There's a blockage inside," said Jim, peeling off plastic, skin thin gloves. "We had better give him a drench. I'll get a stomach tube."

Afterwards Rob knew that he would never forget that day. The tube was slowly pushed up Snowman's nose while he stood legs braced, eyes wild.

"Why don't you come inside? They don't need you. Your Dad can manage," Rob's mother pleaded.

But he had to stay. He had to see it through, for

33

right from the moment when he had walked Snowman home, he had become his responsibility and he wasn't going to shirk it now.

"Swallow the tube, come on, swallow it," Jim said, but Snowman clenched his teeth and remained stubborn. Then his nose started to bleed and blood spattered the walls and Dad's suit. It was like a tap with blood inside turned full on. Jim gave Snowman another injection to stop the bleeding. After that he fetched a bottle from his car and poured the drench down Snowman's throat the old fashioned way. Then he went inside to wash, grim-faced.

"Your wife rang," Rob's mother said, clattering saucepans.

"I thought she would," Jim said sounding downcast. As he started his car Rob's father said, "Your wife will read the riot act."

"What are we meant to do now?" asked Rob standing helplessly in the yard.

"Give Snowman a nice mash later. Come on, let's enjoy our dinner; it's waited long enough." His father washed at the sink. Dinner was on the table in the room they called the Dining Room, though they hardly ever ate there, for most of the year the large table was covered with papers—bills in red, circulars, THE FARMER'S WEEKLY. But Mrs Bartrum had cleared it all away for Christmas.

Rob felt very tired now, but the sense of boredom which had hung over him for years was gone, for ever since the arrival of Snowman every day had been peppered by hope and despair.

After lunch Rob's parents sat by the open fire in

the low-ceilinged sitting room and fell asleep. Rob went outside to look at Snowman, who was standing at the back of his stable looking drowsy. Everything was still again, not a plane overhead, nor the sound of a car in the distance. My tenth Christmas, thought Rob, and it has been quite different than all the others. A Christmas to remember.

When he returned indoors his mother was making tea. "How is he?"

"All right, I think."

"He's going to get well. Don't you worry son. I see it in his eye. He's got the will to live; it's when an animal gives up you're finished, there's no hope then," his father said waking up with a start. Rob's father knew about horses, because years ago his own father had kept a few work-horses on his farm, preferring them to tractors. Sometimes Rob's father had ridden them home in the evening, after they had finished work, perched on top of the harness. Rob knew that, because there was a photograph of him doing it, a broad-faced, smiling boy on a gigantic horse.

Rob took a warm mash out to Snowman later on and gave him some hay. He was eating now and he wasn't sweating any more.

"What's did I tell you," his father said feeding his pigs. "He's what we call out of the wood, or on the mend. He's going to be all right now, you'll see."

"I'm sorry about having the vet out on Christmas Day," Rob said. "Will he be angry for ever?"

"No, it's all in a day's work," his father replied. "And we'll manage."

And Rob knew that was all they had been doing for the last three years—just managing, without buying new clothes, nor having a holiday, just working day in, day out. And he thought I'm not going to be a farmer when I'm grown up. I'm going to study and become an accountant and then I'll know how to manage my own money.

He took away Snowman's empty feed bucket and washed it. He rugged up Snowman and, leaving him with plenty of hay and water, went indoors again.

"I think he's going to be all right now Mum. Do you think I'll be able to ride him soon?" he asked.

"Not yet. And I think you should have some riding lessons first Rob," she said. He saw himself having riding lessons, listening to remarks about his leg; then advised to go to Riding for the Disabled which was free.

Laying the table for supper he thought, I'm not having lessons, I'm going to get a book and teach myself. It'll be a secret between me and Snowman. We'll practise when Mum's out working and Dad's feeding the pigs. I'll do it in secret until I can really ride. And in his imagination he saw his parents standing together staring at him, then calling out, "But you can ride Rob." And it wouldn't have cost anyone a penny.

Chapter Four

THE EARS OF A MULE

A few days later Sarah appeared in the farmyard with a friend called Jane. Jane was fat and spotty with curly red hair and a pale complexion. They were both mounted, Sarah on a dark grey called Squirrel, Jane on a chestnut called Redskin.

Snowman was turned out in the small paddock near the house. On seeing the other ponies, he raised his head and whinnied, which brought Rob from the house pulling on an anorak and struggling into boots as he hurried.

Seeing him Sarah called, "He's still alive then?"

Jane looked at Rob and smirked. Fat and spotty, she was used to being teased and liked to tease back whenever she had the chance, so that now she said, "Your pony is a walking skeleton and he's got a ewe neck, sickle hocks, a goose rump and the ears of a mule, or haven't you noticed, Rob?"

She sounded as though she had prepared the statement and was now delivering it at a meeting.

Both girls had dismounted. There was a short silence before Rob replied, "It doesn't bother me. I don't care how he looks, it's all the same to me." And now old fat Pippa appeared barking shrilly at the visitors.

"And she's so fat she can hardly waddle," Jane added obviously enjoying herself.

"Shut up. Just shut up," Sarah said.

Rob leant down and patted Pippa whom he loved but not as much as he loved Snowman.

Fortunately Rob's mother appeared then, crying "Oh visitors. How lovely! Do you want to tie your ponies up and come inside?" smiling with pleasure as she spoke, then adding, "Come in and have some gingerbread. I've just made a batch."

The two girls smiled at one another and ran up their stirrups, loosened their girths; then picked up some binder twine and tied their ponies to the fence. "They're my aunt's ponies," explained Sarah (who became a different person when she was talking to Rob's mother.) "I hope they'll be all right."

"What a lovely house, it's so warm and cosy. Shall we take off our boots?" asked Jane.

"And doesn't the gingerbread smell divine," added Sarah.

"Come in Rob, don't hover outside like a ghost," said his mother.

"Come on in, all of you. It's not often we have visitors, especially Rob. It really is a treat." And Rob's mother smiled at the girls again, while Rob's mind kept repeating to him the words—ewe neck, sickle hocks, a goose rump and the ears of a mule.

"I do love your kitchen Mrs Bartrum, it's so home-ly," beamed Jane.

And his mother lapped it up, all smiles, offering

more and more gingerbread until the whole lot had gone, muttering to Rob, "Don't be so glum love, cheer up," more than once.

"Thank you so much, that was lovely but we really must be going now," said Sarah at last.

"Yes, it was fantastic. I won't need any lunch now," added Jane.

"What do you think of Snowman? Is he improving?" asked Rob's mother.

"He's a walking miracle, but he's still got a long way to go," replied Sarah sounding like an expert.

"But you think he will recover?"

"Oh yes, in a year or two," replied Jane with a smirk.

Then they both giggled and went outside, while Rob's mother took the empty cake plate to the sink saying, "I'll have to make another lot now. Never mind, they did enjoy it, didn't they?"

And Rob wondered why his mother had to feed people so much, why it was always, 'come in, have some coffee, have a biscuit, help yourself.' He watched Sarah and Jane untie their ponies and ride away in silence.

"Why didn't you go out and give them a hand, or at least wave goodbye. Look they're waving to you," his mother said watching them leave from the window. "No wonder you have no friends if you behave like that, Rob. And they seem such lovely girls and Sarah's the Rector's daughter, not just anyone, Rob."

"You don't know what they're like, or what they said," Rob answered after a moment.

"What did they say, come on tell me."

"You wouldn't understand."

"Yes, I would. I'm not a fool Rob. Come on tell me, please."

Rob looked at his mother and thought, she's so kind and gullible, she doesn't understand, and never will, and if I tell her she'll be hurt too and what's the point of hurting two people.

"They were rude about Snowman," he said putting on his boots again.

"But they didn't mean it," his mother said. "They were joking."

"When are you going shopping, because I want a book about stable management and riding," Rob said, changing the subject.

"But your Dad knows about stable management," she said.

"Not everything Mum, nobody knows everything. I mean does he know what a goose rump is or a ewe neck? I bet he doesn't Mum."

"Is it important?"

"Yes."

Rob was filled with hate now. He had hated Bill and now he was hating Sarah and Jane and Ann Casting and he felt poisoned by it, because continuous hate poisons everything. Food tasted different and every time he looked at Snowman instead of seeing improvement, he found only fault. He bought a book and looked up the words Jane had used and found them, and he knew now what they meant— ewe neck was a neck which was concave instead of convex. Goose rump was a rump which sloped too quickly and sickle hocks were described as 'bent and weak-looking hocks which somehow resemble a drawn out sickle in shape,' and as for his ears, well everyone knows that mule ears are almost as long as donkey ears!

He told Snowman he didn't care, but however often he said it the words still hurt. And his mother continued talking about Sarah and Jane, telling his father that 'Two lovely girls had called to see Rob,' saying things like, 'Perhaps they'll call again'.

"And eat all the gingerbread again," sneered Rob.

"But I'm sure they'll help you if you need any advice," she continued in her happy encouraging voice, apparently oblivious of his remark. "They must know something about ponies. Don't be so stand-offish love, you'll never make friends that way."

She went to work in the old people's home and came back with gossip about the girls. "Sarah won five rosettes at the local gymkhana last year, and Jane's father is a well-known solicitor whom everyone likes," she told him as though she was giving him some sort of present which should make him happy, or maybe just wishing to prove that she had been right all along in saying they were lovely girls.

School started again. Jane and Sarah went to a different school. Mark had found a new friend so Rob was friendless and tried not to mind. He fed Snowman every morning before he left, turning him out in the paddock afterwards. In the evening he opened the paddock gate and Snowman returned to the stable of his own accord where hay and a feed were waiting. His mother was working all day at the home for the elderly now, and sometimes nights as well.

She had paid the vet's bill and bought Rob some riding boots and a skull-cap. "In the spring you can have riding lessons," she promised. "Because by then we'll be out of the red."

But Rob didn't want to wait until the spring, because by then, Bill who had been sentenced to eight months might be let out early for good behaviour, and Rob wanted to ride Snowman, who was beginning to put on weight at last. But more than anything else in the world, he wanted Snowman to be really his, for ever and ever, beyond all doubt.

January became February. The sun shone and the Crocuses came out under the trees in the garden in front of the farmhouse.

One day when Rob's mother was working and his father in the top meadow harrowing, Rob caught Snowman and knotting the headcollar rope so that it became reins, scrambled onto his back off the field gate. Patting Snowman, he said, "Walk on," and then he was riding triumphantly, rather slowly it's true, but riding just the same. He had studied his book on riding and now discovered that his injured leg would not do what it was told, and insisted on staying with its toe down rather than up. Otherwise riding seemed easy and Snowman did everything he could to help. Getting off, Rob gave him an apple. I've done it, he thought. I can ride. After that Rob practised riding every evening and soon his parents found out and told him it was all right as long as he stayed in the paddock for the time being.

Later when everything had gone wrong they said that he had agreed to this. "You gave a solemn promise," his mother said. "You accepted what we said," his father insisted. "Now we can't trust you any more," added his mother. But all that was later, when things had gone wrong, and Rob had lost all confidence and the future appeared as bleak as the bleakest day.

Now, he rode evening after evening. He put markers around the paddock and steered Snowman between them. He studied his book and sat straight up and looked between Snowman's huge ears which now, because he was fatter, looked smaller. And at night he dreamed he was galloping across fields on Snowman, or standing in a ring receiving a prize. After these dreams he woke in the morning full of hope, and the spring, which was coming, seemed to enforce this hope, with birds making nests in eaves of the house, hens laying, trees breaking into leaf and best of all new grass breaking through the tired winter earth.

Snowman began to lose his winter coat. The blacksmith had trimmed his hoofs for the third time. His eyes shone, his quarters filled out, the lines in his haunches disappeared, his neck grew thicker.

At this time an Asian boy called Arif joined Rob's class at school. He was brilliant at maths and wore glasses. He and Rob became friends. He helped Rob with his homework and did his father's VAT returns for him. He didn't play games either and didn't mind. In fact he hated games, so they spent a lot of time together. Rob stopped hating Sarah and Jane. He forgot his limp which Arif never mentioned. He grew and became stronger. His work at school improved.

43

He moved into higher sets.

March became April, the wind blew and howled like a deranged beast. The tiles blew off the house roof, fallen branches blocked the lane. A fox carried off three of the hens. Snowman hated the wind. He was strung up and nervous and ready to bolt at the least sound.

"Don't ride him in the paddock until the wind's gone," said Mrs Bartrum wisely. She was busier than ever, sometimes Rob hardly saw her all day, even on a Saturday. But they were out of debt now, and the spring wheat was up and the barley doing well. The only smudge on their horizon was the thought that quite soon Bill might be let out of prison and return to claim Snowman. But now, as Rob's mother kept saying, "We have enough money to buy him." She had promised Rob a set of tack on his birthday which was on 14th April. "Then you must join the Pony Club and have proper lessons," she said. "That will be lovely won't it? You'll make lots of friends that way."

And Rob wondered, not for the first time, why she thought to have friends was so important. His best friend was Snowman, closely followed by Arif, who sadly did not care for animals and always washed his hands after touching Pippa as if she were somehow infectious. That was the only thing Rob didn't like about his friend—the feeling he gave that animals were unclean. And in his turn Arif couldn't understand Rob's love for Snowman. Rob's mother liked Arif and felt confident in leaving them alone together. "He looks like a real owl behind his glasses but a very clever one," she was fond of saying. And his father agreed, saying that anyone who could understand VAT returns must have a first rate brain in his head.

So everything looked set fair and then Rob spoilt it all.

Chapter Five

GO FIND ROB

Arif wasn't there that evening. Rob came home from school alone. His mother was waiting for him. "Tea's on the table. I've got to go and see to the elderly folk. Your father's working in the top field. Don't do anything silly Rob," she said looking at him.

She always called the people at the home the elderly folk. She was fond of all of them, even the most difficult. She had an excuse for anything they did wrong; in fact in her eyes they could do no wrong. Rob looked at her and wanted her to stay. He didn't want to eat tea alone. He wanted her there fussing over him, saying, "How was school?" Though he might not have bothered to reply, he wanted her there just the same. In spite of that he said, "It's all right. I've got Snowman. He needs a good groom. He's losing his coat."

"Dad will be down here soon. Take care," his mother said. She was wearing an overall under her winter coat. She rode away on her bike and Pippa watched her go before returning indoors with a defeated look on her face.

Rob had done most of his homework returning home on the bus. He didn't feel like tea. The sky was full of dark, dancing clouds. He reckoned he had time for a quick ride before it was dark; but he knew he would have to hurry. Rob felt that time was running out as he changed into jeans and a thick sweater. He often felt like that, for he was constantly counting the days until Bill would be out of prison and maybe demanding Snowman's return. He knew what his parents would say then. His father would say, "Well we did our best and no-one can do more than that." His mother would cry. Then she would wipe her eyes and make the best of it. After that she would work twice as hard, so that they could buy him another pony, one which was really his, which no-one could take away. But Rob didn't want another pony; he wanted Snowman, nothing else. He pulled on his wellington boots and went outside. He caught Snowman and groomed him. And it was still light which seemed a miracle after the long dark winter. He could hear the tractor working the top field. The clouds were growing darker and moving faster as he mounted Snowman off the gate.

Rob was used to riding bareback now. It was obvious that once long ago Snowman had been well schooled, and even in a headcollar he would rein back and stop and start without any trouble. But now he was becoming bored with the same old routine. Snowman kept stopping to look towards the stable, as though trying to say, 'Isn't it time I went inside'. Then he stopped at the gate and Rob was certain that he was saying, 'Let's go outside, just for a change.' Rob thought of the bridleway which led over the hill and then through a wood. Because of his

47

leg he had never been there. Now he was overcome by an overwhelming desire to see it properly. He pushed Snowman up to the paddock gate, unlatched it. "We won't go far; just as far as the wood Snowman, just for a change. Okay?" he asked. Snowman nudged the gate open with his nose. "Just to please you," Rob added.

Snowman raised his head and smelt the air. And still the clouds danced in the sky. Rob felt dusk descending as he left the farm behind. He could hear the tractor still working in the top field. And now Rob was doing what he had been told not to do a dozen times or more, but he told himself that his mother was over-protective, that he wasn't a small boy any more, that sooner or later he had to break free. Besides he was tired of being careful all the time. The wind softly touched his face as he rode past Mark's home and he could see things he had never noticed before on foot or car. Rob felt like a Prince now. Snowman was careful. He was thrilled to be out, but he wanted to be good. In spite of that, to Rob sitting on top, he felt quite different—a changed pony with a spring in his step, pricked ears, cheerful eyes, arched neck. He felt bigger and finer.

Soon Rob could see the village below them; the church, the Rectory where Sarah lived; the only shop; the Haven where his mother worked. He felt happy in a way he had never felt happy before. He felt as though he were king of all he surveyed. They reached the wood, which would soon be deep in bluebells. Here tall, straight beech trees raised their heads to the darkening sky. The first drops of rain began to fall.

"We'll have to turn back," said Rob regretfully, but went on just the same. Snowman didn't want to turn back either; Rob could feel it in his stride. After years on a tether and weeks on the farm, he too wanted change.

They trotted through the last of the wood and reached a track which ran beside a ditch and led to Dyson's Farm. It was all new to Rob. He felt like Snowman—suddenly free. He looked at his watch. "In five minutes we'll have to turn back," he told Snowman patting his neck. The old grey pony shook his head and hurried on. He didn't want to go back either—not yet, not until he had reached the farm below.

The sky was darker now, the clouds were shifting into clusters, joining together, turning the sky black and stormy. Suddenly everything seemed quiet. Rob thought of Arif, who so much enjoyed helping his father with his business affairs when he might have been outside walking or riding. Then he thought of Sarah and how life might have been had they followed her aunt's advice. He thought, soon I will have a saddle and bridle; then I'll be able to join the Pony Club if they will have me. And suddenly everything seemed possible, likely even and he wanted to go on riding for ever and ever. He didn't want anything else at that moment, just to ride on and on across the darkening landscape with Snowman's grey ears and his thin grey neck, topped by his straggly grey mane in front. Then Rob started to daydream about the future; to imagine rosettes, his and Snowman's pinned to his bedroom wall. He did not need perfect legs to ride, he knew that now. When he was on Snowman his disability simply vanished, was forgotten, didn't matter any more. He thought of Arif again who did not like animals and was suddenly appalled. And because Rob's mind was so far away, he was not ready for what happened next. One moment he was daydreaming, the next in the air, then falling into space. It was nobody's fault. Afterwards his mother was to call it fate, whereas his father would say angrily that if Rob had done as he was told, it would never have happened, but that was later when the worst was over. What happened now, happened very quickly; one second Snowman and Rob were together, the next something had leapt from the grass and was between Snowman's hoofs—a rabbit, a bird, no-one knew what, not even Snowman, who leapt in the air instinctively with no thought for Rob on his back. And then they were both in the ditch which ran alongside the track, both struggling to get out. Rob hadn't a chance. Snowman's hoofs hit his head and then there was nothing but blackness. Snowman climbed out of the ditch. For a second he hesitated, then threw up his head and galloped homewards neighing wildly in distress, while the dark clouds burst in the sky and the storm broke.

Melanie Bartrum wheeled her bike into the farmyard. She was wet through. There was neither a light on in the house, nor a yard light which made her know at once that something was wrong. Her husband was driving down from the top field, tractor lights blazing. She waved to him and shouted, "Where's Rob, Charlie?" but he couldn't hear her above the sounds of falling rain and tractor's engine.

She called "Rob, Rob where are you?" while alarm bells started to ring in her head. Charlie Bartrum was smiling. He had finished drilling the top field just a few minutes after the storm broke. He too was wet, but it was nothing compared to the relief he felt at having finished the job which had been hanging over him for days. All he wanted now was a cup of tea and a warm fire to sit by. But Melanie was waving and shouting for she had found Snowman waiting by his stable, soaked through, with a scratched knee. But no Rob. Her heart was hammering inside her like a piston engine working at full blast.

"Where's Rob? You were supposed to be keeping an eye on him," she screamed.

Charlie Bartrum got off his tractor heavily. "What do you mean, where's Rob?" he asked, in his slow uncomplicated voice, which now infuriated his wife.

"Where's Rob, I'm asking you, where is he? Don't you know? You were here," she cried beside herself with worry.

She was putting Snowman into his stable as she spoke. She looked half drowned, tired, disheartened, furious, anxious, all mixed together. "Where is he? Wake up man," she screamed. "Where did he go? or didn't you notice?"

And now alarm bells were ringing in his head too. "I'll get the Land Rover out. He must have gone out

51

on Snowman. I didn't see him go." Charlie Bartrum felt guilty now. He had been so happy finishing the top field. He had felt triumphant. Now he knew he had let down his wife and son.

"I can't wait for you. I'll go up the bridleway. He must have gone that way, and I told him again and again." Melanie Bartrum shouted, but she could not remember what she had told Rob. Not to go out until he had a saddle and bridle? That's what she had said, yes, that was it, she remembered now, running towards the bridle-path, her overall still on under her wet coat, her lace-up plastic shoes soaked through.

Automatically, without thought, Charlie Bartrum gave Snowman an armful of hay and checked that he had water before he set off in the Land Rover. It was still raining on and on as though it would never stop. The lights were dimmed by it, the road outside running with it, and lying somewhere was Rob, unless he had sought cover and left Snowman to gallop home alone. But then he would have telephoned, yes surely he would have telephoned, decided Charlie Bartrum. Obviously the old pony had come home seeking help, and there had been no-one there. For some time now he had hated his wife going out to work, seen it as a sign of failure on his part to earn more money, to keep her and Rob in comfort; for he was old fashioned enough to think that a mother should be at home. And now steady, dour, salt of the earth Charlie Bartrum felt like crying and he had not cried since his mother had died.

Melanie stood in the wood now calling, "Rob, Rob

where are you? Answer me please. Rob, it's your mother, where are you love?" Her voice was plaintive while all around her the tall beech trees dripped rain. Everything was dark and she had forgotten to bring a torch. So soon she had to turn back, for night had descended, black and wet, a night she would never forget.

She found Charlie Bartrum in the house. "I've telephoned Jim Drake at Dyson's Farm. He's seen nothing," he said twisting his wet cap between his hands, not meeting her eye, ashamed.

"I wish Rob had never set eyes on the pony. I do really. He's bewitched by it," shouted Melanie Bartrum.

"He felt like a king on it," replied Charlie Bartrum with a flash of understanding.

"Who wants to be a king?" shouted Melanie.

"Most of us at some time or other. Come on and get a torch, we'll go up the bridleway in the Land Rover," said Charlie Bartrum.

"I've got a better idea," said Melanie Bartrum. "Let's let the old pony go. He may lead us to Rob. He's clever enough."

"Yes we could give it a try."

So they opened the stable door and pulled a steaming Snowman outside by the mane. Then Rob's mother cried, "Go find Rob," as though the old pony with the haggard face was a dog, a sheep dog most likely.

Snowman lifted his head and neighed. "He's calling to him," said Charlie Bartrum.

His wife did not answer, for she was praying

53

silently without moving her lips, but praying just the same.

Then the haggard old pony tossed his head and set off down the drive at a canter, and the Bartrums leapt into the Land Rover and, with blazing lights, followed. Charlie Bartrum was thanking God that Snowman was almost white, because otherwise they would have lost him in the blackness and the pouring rain; while Melanie Bartrum was thinking he's doing his best poor old pony, but what if he doesn't lead us to Rob?

Strangely at that very moment Sarah was discussing Rob with her mother, saying that in spite of his leg, he was going to make a good rider, she felt it in her bones.

Meanwhile, Rob had come round, and was trying to turn himself over and scramble out of the ditch without success. He was very wet by this time and very cold; his teeth were chattering, while the rest of him felt numb. And he was very frightened, more frightened than he had ever been before. He wanted to shout, but no sound came when he tried, and everything was black with night and wet with rain.

Rob was afraid now that he would never get out alive. Ten minutes later, he was beyond caring. Someone had told him once, probably his grandfather when he was still alive, that was how it was in wars; in the end you were brave because you didn't care what happened to you any more. He had said nothing really mattered then, so you went on regardless. And now Rob felt burning hot and he thought, when you die of cold you are hot first, just before you die. He wondered how anyone would find him on a pouring wet night half buried in a ditch. Next he thought, I'll never learn to ride properly now. I'll never show anyone what I can do, in spite of my leg. It's all too late. Why didn't I listen? Why didn't I stay in the paddock just a little longer? Just till my birthday and the new saddle and bridle which I know Mum's buying me, though she thinks it's still a secret. He thought that now he might never see the saddle and bridle and he said to himself, if I get out of here alive, I'll never complain again about anything.

After that he thought how sensible Arif was, because he never did anything reckless, was never caught by rain without a raincoat, never forgot his packed lunch for school, read and read, studied all day long, so that one day he would be rich and respected. Other boys laughed at him. They called him a swot and boring. But Arif didn't mind, just said, "You wait and see. When you're out of work, I will be prospering."

But now Rob could hear the sound of an engine in the distance and soon it was crashing through the wood. Then its lights made pools of yellow in the grass above him. He tried to call, but no sound came from his lips, though his teeth chattered as loudly as a clattering typewriter. Then Rob heard a snort, smelt wet pony above him in the night, wet grey pony which smelt more like a wet white hen than anything else. The engine stopped. His father was saying, "Whoa, steady Snowman. Good pony," in the slow voice he used to animals which was somehow comforting and firm at the same time.

Then Rob felt rather than saw a flashlight shining on his back, while his mother cried, "Oh my God!" thinking he was dead.

And Rob wanted to say, "I'm all right," which was not true of course, but might have comforted her, except that his chattering teeth prevented him from saying anything.

"What if his back's broken?" she whispered, while his father said, "We've got to get him out. There's a rug in the Land Rover. Get it will you?"

Smelling of the farm and wet Husky, Rob's father clambered into the ditch. "How are you son?" he asked, and then, "We'll have you out in a jiffy, just hang on a few minutes longer." And his voice made Rob feel suddenly safe. They'll get me out and take me home, he thought, and that was all he wanted at that moment, just to be safe and warm and comforted.

Meanwhile Snowman stood silently tossing his head in the dark, and the rain went on falling.

They got Rob out in the end wrapped in the rug from the Land Rover. Charlie Bartrum slapped Snowman on the rump and told him to go home, while Melanie Bartrum tried to control her tears. And Rob said not a word; because being moved had been so painful that he had passed out for a second time.

"We should have had a doctor first. He should have had morphine. Goodness knows what damage we've done," cried Melanie Bartrum.

Snowman was galloping now back through the wood, along the track churned to mud by the wheels of the Land Rover. He was going to the farm which was the only place he called home. He did not hesitate. Like a phantom in the night he passed by Mark's cottage, then galloped up the drive to where the farm stood still in the dark driving rain.

Chapter Six

A LONG NIGHT

Rob was conscious again. There were lights everywhere and a smell of antiseptic. Rob's mother had left her coat and overall in the Land Rover, but was still wearing her plastic work shoes which she hated. His father's coat dripped water onto the polished floor. Nurses took Rob to a cubicle, undressed him bit by bit, gently cutting away the boot which encased his right leg which was swollen. He knew the hospital—he had been there before, so wasn't afraid. Able to talk again, he grew warmer and his teeth stopped chattering. He kept saying the same thing: "Is Snowman all right?"

"Yes, fine," his mother said.

"It wasn't his fault."

"I know," she said. She told Rob's father to go away. "You must see to the animals. I can manage all right," she said sitting down on a chair in the corner of the cubicle.

Hating hospitals, Charlie Bartrum was relieved to go. "I'll telephone later," he said. "Just to see how he is."

"You do that," replied Rob's mother. "But don't ring before nine. All right?"

"Who is Snowman?" asked a nurse after a time.

58

"A pony," Rob's mother answered.

"Another riding accident," said the Doctor who had just arrived on the scene. "Why do children have to ride?"

"I don't know. I suppose it's in their blood," replied Rob's mother sitting primly with her hands folded in her lap.

"Rugby and football are just as bad," suggested a nurse smiling at Rob.

Rob's breathing sounded like a rasp working on a horse's hoof. He had a dislocated hip and was bruised all over. He would have to stay in, the Doctor said. And might have to stay in for some time, it all depended on his chest which would be X rayed in the morning. Rob was wheeled away and put to bed. He was injected with pain killer, sedatives and antibiotics. Soon he stopped asking "Is Snowman all right?" He lay in bed with his chest going in and out like bellows. His mother was told she could stay the night if she so wished, an offer she accepted with hesitation. Outside it had stopped raining.

Snowman's stable door had slammed shut in the wind and rain. Charlie Bartrum found him standing shivering with cold in the yard. He put him inside, dried him with straw, wishing all the time that Rob had never set eyes on him. Then he went inside to feed Pippa. He was very tired. Pippa wouldn't eat anything. She looked at him with disappointed eyes before curling up in her basket with her back to him, wanting Melanie. Rob's uneaten tea was still on the kitchen table. His school books were flung down on a chair in the living room, his school blazer hanging on the bannisters. Charlie Bartrum wished now that he had stayed in the hospital.

He went outside again and put a rug on Snowman. The rain had stopped; the yard was running with water. His bones ached from sitting so long on the tractor. He didn't want to return to the house empty now except for Pippa. Later he rang the hospital. Rob was comfortable; there was no other news. Charlie Bartrum wished it was morning already as he went upstairs for a wash. He recalled Snowman leading them to where Rob lay; he had never known a horse to do that before, it was almost a miracle.

"Is Snowman all right?" Rob woke up at three o'clock in the morning and asked that question again and again. His mother was not there to answer him. The nurse thought he was concussed and called the Doctor on duty.

"Now go to sleep young man, and forget all about your beastly pony," the Doctor said, leaning over him, bespectacled, in a white coat.

"I only want to know. Why won't anyone tell me?" retorted Rob. "He's dead, isn't he?"

In the end they fetched Rob's mother who appeared in a borrowed dressing gown. "Of course Snowman's all right. He led us to you. He was perfect. He's got a little scratch, that's all. Your Dad went home especially to see to him," she said.

Rob gave a sigh of relief. "That's all right then," he said and slept until at seven a nurse shook him awake to take his temperature, saying, "Wakey, wakey, open your mouth please."

Next morning while Snowman pulled at the short spring grass pushing its way up through the wet earth in his paddock, Rob was wheeled around the hospital to the X-ray department and back again. His bruised, uncomfortable body was examined and discussed. His dislocated hip was put back into place, his temperature taken. Gradually his breathing improved. His hip stopped hurting. He wanted to go home.

Later his parents appeared and told him Snowman was fine. They did not tell him what they had just heard—that Bill was out of prison and wanting his pony back. Rob looked at his mother's worried face. "I'm going to be all right Mum. Everyone says so, so do cheer up," he said. His father stood by the window looking at the concrete path outside. If Snowman goes we'll have to get Rob another pony, a younger one, another grey, he thought. But knew it would take time to find the right one, months maybe, because the choice would have to be just right. Any old pony wouldn't do.

A trolley of warm drinks was brought round. Rob's parents left. Rob slept again. He felt safe now. Everything was going to be all right. In a day or two he would be home again—mended. Things could have been worse, much worse. In future he would be more careful. He knew that now.

Later during that day Sarah and Jane appeared clutching flowers and chocolates. Looking down at

Rob, Sarah said, "Are you going to be all right? We were so worried when we heard what had happened. We rode round to see you and you weren't there. It was horrific!"

"But Snowman was there, wasn't he?" asked Rob anxiously.

"Yes of course," Sarah said at exactly the same moment as Jane.

"He was all right then?" inquired Rob.

"Yes, fine." They found chairs and chatted. Rob was tired now and wanted to sleep, but they wouldn't stop talking. They kept on about him joining the Pony Club, and if Snowman was too old, they would find him other mounts, Sarah said.

"He'll never be too old," Rob replied wishing they would go away.

They opened the chocolates they had brought and said, "Do you mind if we help ourselves?"

Rob shook his head.

"You look very pale," Sarah told him eating a chocolate with a nut inside.

They arranged the flowers they had brought in a vase.

"Mum says Snowman showed them where I was, she said it was a kind of miracle. But he knows how much I love him," Rob told them, smiling as though Snowman was a child and he, his proud father.

They looked at one another and nodded. He was sitting up now and could see the sun shining on the concrete paths outside, and he wanted to be at home.

In the afternoon a Get Well card arrived from Arif. On the front was a gorilla swinging on a tree. The gorilla was saying, "I'm going to get you out right now." Inside Arif had written, ALL THE BEST ARIF.

His mother came in the evening. She said, "Everything's fine. Not to worry."

She was wearing her overall under her coat again. She was going straight to work afterwards, and didn't stay long.

"I want to go home tomorrow. Do you think they'll let me out?" Rob asked as she left.

She nodded and smiled and waved.

After she had gone Rob lay in bed remembering the ride. How wonderful Snowman had felt beneath him, so full of life. Rob knew that the old pony was growing fitter and more handsome every day so that in time he might even be a show pony.

A nurse smiled at him. "You look happy," she commented.

"I am, but I want to go home," he said.

She patted his hand and murmured, "Just one more day love."

Rob liked the nurses and they seemed to like him. But still there was only one thing he wanted—to go home. He wanted to pat Snowman and tell him that he had saved his life. Rob didn't really care now whether he won prizes or not. He just wanted to be well again and to ride for miles and miles, for ever and ever. Soon Rob fell asleep and when he wakened, the curtains were drawn across the windows and another day was gone.

Tomorrow I'll be home. I must be. I feel miles better, thought Rob. Snowman will whinny when he sees me, and Pippa will go mad. Mum will have made a special meal. And the nightmare will be over.

Soon a nurse brought a bowl of water to his bed. "Here I'll wipe your face," she said. "Then you can clean your teeth. Tomorrow you can get up and have your lunch over there at the table. That'll be nice won't it?"

"But tomorrow I'm going home," Rob replied.

"Who told you that?"

"I can't remember."

"Well not me or Doctor. We've got to get the fluid off your chest first," the nurse said. "We mustn't send you home too soon, or you'll be back in no time, and you wouldn't like that, would you?" she asked smiling.

Rob felt too cast down to answer. "But I thought . . ." he began, after a moment.

"Well, you thought wrong dear, you're not out of the wood yet," replied the nurse. And then of course he thought of the wood, where the trees stood so tall and straight and he wanted to be there again riding Snowman. Quickly he wiped tears from his eyes, while the nurse told him he was tired and that time would soon pass. She re-arranged his pillows and straightened his sheets and all the time he was aching for the wood and Snowman, and the ache would not go away. Later he dreamed he was riding again, galloping across the sunlit fields, and Sarah was there and said to him, "Snowman's good enough to jump for England." His heart gave a great leap of joy which woke him. And after that, he couldn't sleep again.

"Well you can't have him. We nursed him back to

health and he's here to stay," said Charlie Bartrum in a loud voice.

"We'll buy him. How much do you want? Just name your price," said Melanie.

Bill had appeared. Ever since they had heard that he was out of prison they had been expecting him. Now he was standing in front of them, unshaven, belligerent, smelling of drink, carrying an old hemp halter in a surprisingly clean hand. Snowman was standing nervously at the back of his box.

"We'll have you put in prison for neglecting him," threatened Charlie Bartrum.

"We had to nurse him back to health. It cost a fortune. If Rob hadn't brought him here, he would have died. And now while the poor boy's in hospital, fighting for his life, you come to take him away. It beggars description," cried Rob's mother.

"Well, if your boy's going to die, he won't want him, will he?" replied Bill with dreadful callousness.

Charlie Bartrum wanted to hit him. He wanted to knock him down and stamp on him. He wanted to pick him up and throw him outside the farmyard. He wanted to kick him over and over again. Suddenly he was frightened of his feelings which he was fighting to control. And he had never felt that way before.

Melanie was standing in front of the stable door. "You can't have him. You'll have to kill me first," she said.

Bill looked at them with contempt. "I'll have to get the police I suppose," he said. "Then I'll have you put inside for theft."

"That's rich, you fetch the police. That's the joke of the year," cried Rob's father.

"Yes, He's my pony. He's for my little girl," Bill replied.

"But you haven't got a little girl. It's all in your imagination," cried Melanie Bartrum. "Where is she? You're too old to have a little girl, Bill."

"She'll always be my little girl, to me that is," replied Bill stubbornly. "I'll be back with the police, you'll see. I want my pony back."

They watched him walk away. When he reached the road he turned around to call again, "I'll be back."

"The police won't help him," said Charlie Bartrum scornfully.

"We can't be sure," replied Melanie fetching Snowman a handful of oats. "And I'm so frightened, frightened for Rob, I mean. Losing Snowman will kill him."

"Rob's not that soft," replied Charlie Bartrum, but he wasn't sure, because love had killed people before, everyone knew that, and Rob really loved Snowman.

"I'm not going to work. I'm staying put. How I wish we had a big dog Charlie, instead of silly old Pippa," complained Melanie.

"You can't intimidate people with dogs, it's not allowed," replied her husband. "I'll stay around too. I'll be in the cow-sheds if you want me and later working on the tractor's engine. I won't go far today."

They looked at each other, two stricken people not sure what to do next. Then Melanie screamed, "Oh I can't bear it," and rushed into the house sobbing wildly, while Snowman whinnied from the stable missing Rob.

Then Sarah appeared saying, "We've seen Rob, he's all right, and Bill's back." Sarah followed Melanie into the house and was embarrassed because Melanie was crying. They sat and drank tea together.

"Surely the police can't take Snowman away?" Sarah said.

But Rob's mother was not sure, was not sure of anything, only knew that if Snowman was taken, Rob's heart would break. "If Snowman goes, Rob will never be the same again. He had such high hopes. He didn't say so, but it was in his eyes. He was a changed person, Sarah," she said.

"I know. But we mustn't be sentimental; there are thousands, no millions of ponies in England," replied Sarah sounding like her aunt.

"It's like love; some people are only capable of falling for one person, no-one else will do," replied Rob's mother pouring tea into their steaming mugs, not really noticing what she was doing, slopping the tea onto the table, fetching a dishcloth to mop it up with, seeing only Rob's face when he returned and found Snowman's stable empty. "Actually I could kill that stupid old man," she added.

"I'm sure the police will be sensible; they usually are," replied Sarah soothingly.

Sarah left. The day dragged on. Snowman grazed in his paddock. The sun shone. The aconites in the garden opened their petals. Mrs Bartrum didn't go to work. She waited for Bill. But he didn't show up, so she had lost a day's pay for nothing. The new saddle and bridle for Snowman waited hidden in the pantry. Hens cackled joyfully, each in turn announcing to the world that they had laid an egg. Charlie Bartrum appeared for tea, talking about local pigs infected with blue ear. The television news told of murder, and of starving millions.

"Perhaps we need a solicitor. After all we have fed Snowman for months," said Melanie. "And we haven't claimed a penny."

But Rob's father didn't believe in solicitors. "They charge you a mint of money for doing nothing," he snapped back.

Meanwhile Snowman snatched hay from his haynet, then looked out into the yard still missing Rob. He kicked over his bucket of water and dropped much of his hay over his stable door. He felt lonely and deserted. If he could not have Rob, he wanted another horse to keep him company.

The next day two policemen called. Rob's mother was at work. His father shook the two policemen by the hand, ignoring Bill who stood behind then with a gleam of satisfaction in his small mean eyes.

"I'm afraid you will have to let the pony go. I know it's hard for you Mr Bartrum, but in the eyes of the law he belongs to this gentleman here," the tallest policeman said.

Gentleman! Some Gentleman! thought Charlie Bartrum.

"You know how my boy found him? He was starving," he said. "Also, a few more hours and he would have been dead."

"That isn't relevant. You should have called us instead of taking the law into your hands, Sir," replied the tallest policeman.

"It was snowing. You couldn't have got here. We were cut off. And that old man was in custody."

"He's ready to pay you for what you did," the smaller policeman said. "Just name the price."

"I'm not interested in the old tramp's money. But you're not taking the pony, not until my son's home," shouted Charlie Bartrum. "I've put a padlock on the stable door. And I tell you, you're not having him, so will you kindly leave?"

But now Charlie Bartrum was quite incapable of seeing sense. He could only see the grief on Rob's face when he found Snowman gone. So looking at Bill he said, "Look, we'll do a swap. You have my tractor and I'll keep the pony. You'll be the gainer then, because it's a good old tractor."

Bill shook his dirty, grizzled head. "I don't want your bleeding tractor," he said.

Afterwards Charlie Bartrum would say that he really did see red at that moment. He was overcome by a feeling of terrible injustice as he hurried to his tractor parked just a few yards away attached to a low loader. Another minute and he was driving it to the gateway, blocking the entrance.

"There you are," he cried switching off the engine and leaping down. Now take the pony away." And with that he stormed into the house locking all the doors after him, half appalled, half triumphant by what he had done, with the tractor's key in his pocket.

"He'll get a gun next. Then we'll have a siege," said the tall policeman glumly. "I hate these domestic incidents."

"You can't leave, not now," said Bill. "You have to see justice done. It's your job."

Meanwhile Snowman walked round and round his loose-box. He wanted Rob. He wanted to be in his paddock. His usual routine was upset and, like most animals, he liked routine. He tossed his head and snorted. He neighed. He broke into a sweat.

"Better send for reinforcements," suggested the tall policeman going to his car.

"If there are any available," replied the other taking off his cap to scratch his ginger hair.

Inside the farmhouse Charlie Bartrum mixed himself a strong drink. "I've got them beat for a moment, but it won't last," he thought. A few minutes later Melanie Bartrum appeared at the farm gate, tired from work.

"What are you all doing here? Has there been an accident?" she cried, alarmed.

"Just a little domestic trouble," replied the tall policeman who was called PC Jones. "Nothing to worry about Madam. This gentleman here has come for his pony, and your husband has blocked the entrance. Perhaps you can make him see sense."

"Sense! What is sense? Here is this filthy old man who has been in prison come to claim his pony, which was dying tethered to a stake in the middle of winter with no shelter whatsoever. He should have been prosecuted then and there, but he was in custody already. We've spent a lot of money saving the pony.

We've nursed him back to health. Now, when our son is lying sick in hospital, you come here demanding the pony back. It's, it's," for a moment she could not find the right word, "insane, unjust, inhumane—it's not justice," she finished furiously.

"We are only attempting to uphold the law love," replied PC Jones.

"And where's my husband?"

"He's barricaded himself into the house unfortunately," replied PC Jones.

"Good for him," cried Melanie Bartrum.

They had reached an impasse, and they all knew it. The two policemen behaved as though they had all the time in the world. Melanie hated them; at this moment she hated almost everyone.

She looked at Bill with fury in her blue eyes. "And you're just scum," she shouted. "The lowest of them all. How could you look after a pony, when you can't even keep yourself respectable? You should have stayed in prison, along with the other good for nothings, that's where you belong, Bill; you're no good to man nor beast; you never have been and never will be. And if you take the pony it will be across my dead body." Melanie Bartrum was shaking with rage by this time. She kept thinking of the saddle and bridle which she had worked for, and might now never be used. Then she imagined Rob's hurt face. His homecoming would be like a wake, a funeral. And she had made a cake for it, his favourite.

"Go and talk to the vets. We had two here to look at Snowman. They'll tell you how he was," she cried.

"That's a different matter altogether. This gentle-

71

man actually owns the pony, love," replied PC Jones.

"Gentleman, you call him a gentleman?" cried Melanie.

"You've owned him for years Sir, haven't you? Ever since he was a foal," continued PC Jones, and Bill replied righteously, "That's right. I bought him for my little girl when she was just a wee thing."

Going towards the house, Melanie wondered why they called Bill 'Sir' and herself 'love'. Until this day she had thought of the police as friends, protectors; now she wasn't sure. Then, as though he read her mind, PC Jones called, "We're only doing our duty, Madam, we can't take sides. We are here to enforce the law."

And Melanie knew that was true, and that made everything seem worse.

"Try and get your husband to come out quietly and move his tractor, or he can give us the key and we will move it. Otherwise we'll have to arrest him for obstruction. He'll be put inside then, and he could get three months," said PC Jones.

And that would only make matters worse, thought Melanie, before calling through the letter-box, "You had better come out Charlie. Maybe we can agree something. Otherwise they'll arrest you. And who will run the farm then?" And now she was crying.

But Charlie Bartrum wouldn't come out. "Tell them to go to the devil. I'm not letting Rob down," was all he said in a voice thick with drink.

There was a small crowd by the gate now, people they all knew. Sarah appeared with her father. The crowd made way for him, because he was their Rec-

72

tor. He was followed by the howling of more police cars approaching, while poor old Pippa barked herself hoarse in the farmhouse and Snowman frantically threw himself against his stable door, knowing that things were happening outside and wanting to know what they were.

Chapter Seven

THE SIEGE

With the police cars came reporters and television cameras. Melanie wondered how the media knew what was happening so soon. Sarah felt desperately sorry for the Bartrums. She doubted whether her father could do any good, but on hearing of a siege at Yew Tree Farm, he had offered to try. It wasn't a real siege, thought Sarah staring round the farmyard, just a blocked drive and a horrid old man demanding his right to a pony he had never looked after.

All the cars, including those of the police, had to park outside the farmyard because of the tractor and trailer. Gradually more and more people appeared to watch the proceedings, mostly with glee. The police kept them out of the yard. "He may have a gun," they said, which only added to the sense of drama and excitement. "A gun! Fancy that, Charlie's got a gun," they murmured to one another, until gradually it became the truth—Charlie Bartrum was inside his farmhouse with a gun. The reporters wrote it down. The television crew filmed everything and asked questions: "What sort of man is he? Has he been in trouble before?" Everyone outside the yard seemed to be enjoying themselves for it wasn't every day they had television filming in the village. Time passed, and the farm animals became restless, as feed time passed unnoticed.

Charlie Bartrum had drunk three-quarters of a bottle of whisky. It had dulled his senses so that even Melanie Bartrum still pleading through the letter-box had little effect.

"Come out Charlie, you're not doing any good. Come out for my sake," she cried.

But the whisky had strengthened his obstinacy and he had no intention of giving in.

Police surrounded the house. Some had guns. "He isn't violent. I tell you he wouldn't shoot anything," pleaded Melanie Bartrum, but to no avail for the police had decided to be safe rather than sorry.

A superintendent wearing stripes on his jacket called through a microphone, "Come out with your hands up, or we'll come in after you Mr Bartrum."

The television crew filmed them, then they filmed the old grey pony who had caused the trouble, frantic in his loose-box. They knew the story now. They knew about Rob lying in hospital. It was a good story. A scoop. The newspaper reporters were having a field day, too. Soon the film crew left, anxious to see Rob so that their work could be on the local TV news that very evening. The police let them climb over the trailer to their cars. Melanie hated them, she hated everyone, Bill most of all, who had given interviews to everyone, telling his interpretation of events. It was enough to make anyone sick, Melanie thought, for Bill had made himself appear to be a man who loved animals, who wouldn't kill a fly. He said that he had gone to prison for a theft so small that it was a joke. And he kept saying, "The pony belongs to my little girl," who everyone knew, if he had a daughter at all, must be at least twenty years old by now. Melanie Bartrum would have wept if she had had any more tears to shed.

Later the TV crew barged straight into the hospital. There was no-one to stop them. Quickly they found Rob and called "Smile" in cheerful voices. Rob was sitting alone in the day room, desperately homesick. "Who are you? What do you want?" he shouted, while their cameras whirred. Staff appeared then and drove them out. But it was too late. The damage was done. Rob had turned pale now and was trembling. "Why are they here? What's happened?" he asked. The nurses didn't know. They soothed him and steered him back to bed. Then one pushed the telephone round to his bedside. "Here ring up home, if it will put your mind at rest," she said.

Rob dialled the familiar number and listened to it ringing. Then he put the receiver down and tried again and felt panic rising inside him as he waited. The nurses told him not to worry. They sat by his bedside while he said, "I want to go home. Why can't I go home? I'm all right now." Then he replaced the receiver and tried to imagine where his parents were, while panic grew inside him.

"We'll see the news. It will be on the news. You can see it in the day room," a young nurse suggested.

Charlie Bartrum let Sarah's father into the house. "I

don't know what to do Rector," he said. He was very drunk.

"Just give me the key and we'll get someone to move the tractor and trailer, and let Bill take his pony home," said Sarah's father. "We'll deal with Bill later. We'll get the pony back. But don't go to prison because it would break your wife's heart," he added.

"It was for Rob," said Charlie Bartrum. "You won't tell him, will you? I don't want anyone to tell him. I'll tell him myself. I'll break it gently."

Sarah's father held out his hand for the key. "Give it to me Charlie. You'll be doing the right thing. We'll get the pony back," he said.

Charlie Bartrum looked like a beaten man as he handed the Rector the tractor key. "You had better have the one to the stable too," he said. And suddenly he wasn't drunk any more. He was as steady as anyone outside, but there was still murder in his heart. "I don't know how it's come to this," he muttered handing over the padlock's key. "I wouldn't have done it for myself, I did it for Rob."

"I know," said the Rector smiling his soothing smile, which women loved and which had healed many a breach and saved many a marriage. "You've done the right thing," said Sarah's father before he stepped outside with the two keys.

A cheer went up then from the people waiting as he held them up, and Bill put his thumbs up in a gesture of triumph, while Melanie Bartrum ran into the house, sobbing uncontrollably.

The police moved the tractor and trailer. Then one of them told Sarah's father that he could call in the morning for a full statement, while another said, "You can have your pony now," to Bill who stood with an ugly look of triumph in his eyes, rehearsing already what he would say in the pub that night, sitting in his corner on the stool he called his own.

Sarah felt rather cold, and now half of her wished that she had not brought her father to mediate. It had seemed the right thing to do at the time, but now she wasn't sure. Beyond the farm gate the newspaper reporters revved up their cars and disappeared. The crowd disbanded talking in excited voices.

In the farmhouse, Pippa threw herself at Melanie Bartrum in a rush of welcome, while she put her arms around her husband and said, "You did your best, no-one can do more than that, Charlie."

Bill unlocked the door of Snowman's stable. The grey pony stood at the back of it, his eyes wild, his body hunched. Bill caught him by the nose and pulled the hemp halter over his grey ears. Then, ignoring Snowman's fear and loathing, dragged him out into the yard.

"You are my pony. You belong to my little girl, and you are coming home," he said yanking on the rope. He walked away along the drive dragging the unwilling pony after him, muttering to himself, "I taught them both a lesson. They won't do that again."

The police were leaving now. The sun had set. Charlie and Melanie set about feeding the waiting animals. They did it automatically, for both their minds were elsewhere. Charlie's pride had been damaged beyond repair. Melanie felt as though her heart was breaking. Leaving, Sarah and her father called, "Can we do anything to help?" and Melanie called, "No thank you," and they both continued filling buckets with water, their backs bent with sorrow and shoulders hunched with despair, wondering how they would break the news to Rob; and, worse still, how they would console him afterwards.

At six forty five Rob saw the farm on television. He saw the police and the crowd and heard the words, " There was a siege today at Yew Tree Farm and all over a pony." He saw his mother; he saw Sarah and her father and heard the newsreader say, "the local Rector, the Reverend Tyler, came to the rescue. And it ended peacefully, Bill has his pony back." And then a picture of himself lying in hospital and the words, "But Rob is still in hospital," and there were many other words Rob did not hear for his head pounded and now he could only think, Snowman's gone. Bill's got him again. And he did not see any more for his eyes refused to focus while in his mind he imagined Snowman being led away, hanging back, being dragged to the same old tether. And tears ran down his face.

"Oh dear, bad news?" the young nurse asked.

Rob did not answer for a moment. Then he said, "I want to go home straight away. I don't want to stay here a moment longer. They've taken away my pony."

"What the one which threw you, well I'm not surprised," the nurse said. "You don't want that sort of pony do you?"

Rob wanted to hit her. Instead he stood up saying,

"I'm going now. I'm not staying here a moment longer. I'm all right."

Another nurse appeared. "Your Mum's just rung. She won't be in this evening. Your Dad's a bit poorly, nothing to worry about, but she thinks she should stay with him. But she will be in first thing to take you home. How's that?" She spoke as though she were offering him a present, but Rob thought it's not good news, it's just another delay while Bill keeps Snowman and nothing's done about it.

In the end a Doctor persuaded Rob to go back to bed. He was a very young Doctor and he said he knew how Rob felt, but Rob knew that wasn't true, because no-one could know how he felt at that moment, stuck in hospital, while Bill kept Snowman and the hours passed and nothing was done about it. No-one else could guess at the terrible despair in his heart. In spite of a sleeping pill, it was hours before Rob slept that night, and then his sleep was wracked by dreams of Snowman lying on the cold earth dying. And when he woke at five and asked to go home, an elderly nurse told him to pull himself together and think of his poor mother who was still asleep. But Rob knew his mother, and he knew that she, like him, would be awake already, her mind in shreds. She would get up weak with worry and make his father a cup of tea in the kitchen which was always warm because of the Rayburn cooker. Pippa would go upstairs with her and climb stiffly onto the bed then sit looking out of the window as dawn broke. While outside the stable would be empty, because Snowman had gone.

Rob did not want breakfast when it came. He only

wanted to go home. It was like a dull pain inside him, which would not go away. He wanted to use the telephone to tell his mother to come at once, but the nurses would not let him have it. "Think of your poor mother. She must be fast asleep," they repeated again and again.

Soon Rob sat in a chair waiting to go home. And the nurses decided to leave him alone there, though he should have washed, and cleaned his teeth and had his temperature taken. They were very busy that morning, so that when Melanie Bartrum appeared at last looking hurt and sad, they hardly noticed.

"I saw it on television," Rob cried when he saw her. "So you don't have to tell me." And then they were both crying.

Rob dressed in the clothes she had brought him and Melanie looked around to thank someone, but everyone seemed so busy she changed her mind. Another minute and they were outside with the signs of spring all around them—budding shrubs, growing grass, dancing sunlight, the sky blue save for a few scuttling clouds. Rob noticed none of it.

"Did Dad really lock himself in the house with a gun?" he asked getting into the familiar car, which smelt of the farm and him.

"Not with a gun," his mother said. "He was trying to keep Snowman. He loves you Rob. He did it for you," she said. "But I don't want to see what they filmed, not ever."

"It was slanted," Rob replied. "It made Bill into a hero, didn't it?"

"I don't know. I didn't see it."

The farm was just the same when they reached it. His father was harrowing Snowman's paddock, sitting on the tractor, his face blank, as though he did not wish to think any more.

"We'll get him back," Rob said to his mother. "Bill's not keeping Snowman. I won't let him."

Melanie Bartrum looked at Rob and sighed. "He's not ours, Rob. We must try and buy him, there's no other way."

"Bill's mad isn't he?" asked Rob after a moment. "And he's a criminal. People like that should not be allowed to have animals."

"Your father could go to prison. We must keep within the law," his mother said, walking indoors, putting the kettle on automatically, seeing nothing but trouble ahead. And hadn't they had enough of it with a son with a wonky leg, she asked herself? And now she was wishing again that Rob had never set eyes on Snowman, that they had let him die alone on his tether. But she knew now that they could not have done it; they couldn't have left him there to die, they had to bring him home. She turned to Rob and said, "We may have to buy you another pony, Rob, however much it costs."

"I've never even sat on the saddle you bought me and isn't it my birthday tomorrow? " Rob asked. And then added, "And Mum I don't want another pony, not ever. Okay?"

Chapter Eight

I DON'T WANT OTHER PONIES

Rob's parents would not let him go to see Snowman that day. They told him that he was too weak, and that someone had said Bill had erected an electric fence so that Snowman was no longer tethered. "And the grass is growing now Rob," his father said sipping tea from a mug, "so he won't die of starvation."

A policeman had called earlier to take a statement from Rob's father. They had called him 'Sir', and told him not to worry. They had asked him to plead guilty.

"But to what?" asked Charlie Bartrum, and refused to plead guilty to anything.

Rob had watched the interview feeling limp and wretched. His mother had offered the policeman coffee or tea but he had refused both. Before he left, Melanie Bartrum asked him why he bothered to protect a criminal like Bill, but the policeman replied that the law applied to everyone, King, Queen, Prince, Princess, teenager or criminal. Then he had left, tucking notebooks into his pockets. After that, Pippa climbed onto Charlie Bartrum's knee trying to console him.

Presently there was a knock on the kitchen door and Sarah walked in. "I rang the hospital, but they said you had left, Rob. Is there anything I can do to help?" she asked.

Melanie Bartrum put the kettle on again, while Rob shook his head glumly. "And I didn't even get to try the saddle Mum has bought."

"We'll find a way, we'll get Snowman back. I'm not giving in anyway," Sarah said. "We won't let Bill keep Snowman. We'll find his little girl and bribe her with sweets. My aunt says everyone has a price. We'll win, Rob. Dad will twist his arm, tell him about hell."

"I don't want pity brought into it. I don't want him back because of my leg. I don't want headlines in the paper saying, 'crippled boy wins pony back'. I couldn't bear it. Okay?" cried Rob, passionately.

"I wasn't thinking along those lines," replied Sarah turning red with embarrassment. "I was just thinking . . .." she stammered so much that Rob knew she was lying.

"My leg is my own business. And I hate pity," he said roughly.

"You're over sensitive about it," replied his mother. "There's far worse things in life than your leg."

"And you only notice it if you look," said Sarah.

"Look and look again. I know," replied Rob bitterly.

"Tea or coffee?" Melanie Bartrum wanted to change the subject.

Charlie Bartrum said, "I must get back to work. There's plenty to do. Don't worry son, we'll get the old pony back." But he went out wearily and heavily thinking that he might go to prison and if he did, how would the farm keep going without him? And then of course he fell to wishing that Rob was really fit, instead of recovering from pneumonia with a gammy leg, and cursed his bad luck in having such a son.

Sarah kissed Melanie Bartrum before she left. "We'll have Snowman back in no time, just trust us," she said shutting the door after her.

"She really likes you, Rob. I can see it every time she looks at you." Melanie Bartrum told Rob, hoping to cheer him up. But now that Rob was home he felt weak and useless; the strength seemed to have left his legs altogether, and when he stood for long he felt weak and faint. And he wanted to be fit. He wanted to help his father. He felt ashamed.

"She's a lovely girl," continued his mother. "I said so right from the start, remember?"

Rob didn't answer. He sat in an armchair with Pippa at his feet. "I don't think we'll ever get Snowman back, and Dad will go to prison and then what will happen?" he asked after a time. "And it will be my fault, won't it Mum?" he added. "I heard the police saying they wanted him to plead guilty. But guilty to what, Mum?"

"Causing an affray, obstructing the police, something like that," replied his mother. "But we will get a good solicitor, we'll be all right, you'll see."

But Rob did not believe her, nor Sarah. He thought, they are both trying to be kind. And he wanted to see Snowman more than anything else.

Later that day Sarah telephoned to say, "I've seen

Snowman. He's all right. He's not tethered; Bill's put up an electric fence and there's a tank full of water. So don't worry too much. Mum has got a great idea. I'll tell you more tomorrow. We'll get him back, never fear."

And all Rob could say, after Sarah had rung off was, "why does she have to get him back, why can't we do it ourselves?"

"Because Bill and your father aren't on speaking terms," his mother replied briskly, peeling potatoes for lunch.

Tomorrow was Rob's birthday. In the afternoon his mother iced a cake and put a horse on it; and then eleven candles. By this time, Rob was asleep upstairs. Next she wrapped up the saddle and bridle in rolls of gift paper which kept tearing. She could not bear to leave him alone in the house, so there was no opportunity to buy him anything else. Various distant relations had sent cards, and an aunt had sent a five pound note. Melanie thought it was not going to be much of a birthday and wished she had time to prepare something better, but it was too late now—they would just have to get through the day as best they could.

Later Rob said, "I hope you are not going to make a fuss tomorrow, because I don't feel like a celebration." And he went outside and looked at Snowman's empty stable, and at the cigarette cartons that reporters had thrown down while they waited, and he felt seeped in misery. Then Rob wanted to smash something, but there was nothing to smash. And he felt too weak to walk up the hill and look at Snowman, and besides he was afraid to meet Bill because he still felt so angry.

Tea was a drawn-out meal. Later Rob ate supper in his dressing gown, near the fire, off a tray on his knee. "You'll be better tomorrow, love, you've been very ill," his mother said, bringing him milk to drink which he did not want, while his father sat going over what had come to be called, The Siege, over and over again in his mind, while Pippa lay snoring under the table.

Rob slept late the next morning. When he went downstairs there was a pile of cards on the table. And a saddle and bridle protruding from wrapping paper. None of it seemed to make much sense. He thought how different it might have been if he had never set out on the fateful ride, and if Bill was still in prison. He looked at the saddle and bridle and said, "It's not much use now is it?" and watched his mother's face crumple and her hands go limp in despair, while his father said, "Don't say that, there's other ponies in the world you know."

"I don't want other ponies," Rob said.

"We know, but sometimes one has to put up with second best," his mother replied wiping her eyes. She had cooked a special breakfast for him. "Aren't you going to open your cards? And look there's a present from Pippa here," she said.

Rob knew that if Snowman had been there she would have bought one from him too. Pippa had given him chocolate, she always did.

"I hate birthdays" he said opening the envelopes

and looking at the cards inside without really seeing them, seeing instead Snowman's haggard face staring over an electric fence longing to be at the farm. And then they heard someone calling, "Happy Birthday Rob. I've got Snowman," They rushed outside and Snowman put up his head and whinnied long and low. Another second and Rob was patting him, and Melanie was fetching a carrot for him and no day had ever been more glorious.

"How did you manage it?" asked Charlie Bartrum staring at Sarah as though she had performed an impossible feat.

Then they saw Sarah's mother driving into the yard in a car smiling and tooting her horn. The next moment she was embracing Rob's mother and saying, "We did it with whisky, once he had three doubles he was ready to sign anything. It was so easy, though his signature is more of a sign than a name. I witnessed it, so we should be safe with Snowman here, for the time being, that is only until his little girl turns up."

"And I'm sure she doesn't exist," cried Sarah gleefully, "because there's not a sign of her anywhere."

And all the time they were talking, Snowman was rubbing his head up and down against Rob, and nickering softly.

"I can't believe it. I just can't believe it," said Melanie Bartrum. "We can try on his saddle and bridle now," said Rob quietly. "This is the best birthday I've ever had." He was still pale-faced, but now his eyes were bright with happiness.

Snowman's box was as he left it. Rob and Sarah

straightened the straw he had churned into the middle as the police cars and Bill had arrived, which suddenly seemed to have happened years ago.

"I'm going to help you Rob," Sarah said. "I will ride over every day and we can school our ponies together. Is that all right with you?"

Rob nodded though he was not sure yet, but he could not object, not now when Sarah had just brought Snowman back.

They tried on the saddle and bridle. Sarah adjusted the bridle. "It's lovely, just right Rob," she said. They were made of dark leather, except for the girth which was white nylon, and the stirrup bits and buckles which were made of stainless steel. "It must have cost your Mum a fortune," Sarah said.

Meanwhile Sarah's mother, Melanie and Charlie Bartrum were looking at the document Bill had signed. It was not long and merely stated that Bill loaned his pony unconditionally to Mr Bartrum until such time that his daughter needed him. But it was witnessed and having been written on a word processor, looked official. Sarah's mother was like her aunt, except that she was kindly rather than formidable, and never spoke before considering the effects her words might have. She admired the farmhouse as they drank coffee together with Rob's cards still lying unloved and unopened on the table. Melanie Bartrum produced a plateful of gingerbread and Sarah's mother said she knew how good it was because Sarah had already told her. Pippa put her head on the visitor's knee and looked at her with soft spaniel eyes.

Later Sarah and Rob groomed Snowman. They fetched him fresh hay and a small feed. Rob felt very weak. He was glad when Sarah and her mother left at last and he was able to sink into a chair in the sitting room. His mother arranged his cards for him on the mantlepiece and kept saying, "They're lovely people, really lovely." Rob thanked her for the saddle and bridle. "They're great and fit perfectly," he said.

Going home, Sarah told her mother that Rob was very weak. "I'm going over to help him tomorrow. I'm going to mark out a dressage arena in Snowman's paddock. We're going to school our ponies together, " she said.

"Well don't overdo it," her mother replied driving up the long weedy drive to the Rectory.

"I want him to join the Pony Club," Sarah continued getting out of the car. "I think he's quite handsome, don't you?"

"Yes, he's a poppet," her mother replied.

Looking at his birthday cards properly for the first time, Rob saw that Arif had forgotten him. But it did not matter any more. He had moved on and now thought of schooling with Sarah and long summer days. At this very moment his father was turning the old dairy into a tack room for him. It was going to be his belated birthday present to Rob.

Snowman looked over his stable door and knew he was home again. He wasn't scared or lonely any more. He felt safe and contented. He had spent hours pacing up and down the electric fence trying to find a way through. He had neighed for Rob again and again in vain. Now the trauma was over. He was back in his own domain with his own roomy stable, bedded deep in straw, and in his own paddock the grass was growing strong and green. So after a time Snowman lay down in the deep straw and slept.

Chapter Nine

DRESSAGE

Next morning Rob's mother said, "I have a feeling we're out of the wood now and everything is going to be all right."

And once again Rob thought of that other wood where he had ridden Snowman in his headcollar, and he shivered. Then he touched the back door just so he could remember that he had touched wood, while his mother said, "Oh Rob don't be so superstitious. With Sarah's parents behind us, I'm sure we'll survive." She had put off going to work at the Home for the Elderly again, for with the saddle and bridle bought, and with Rob's fall still preying on her mind, she was thinking of giving it up altogether.

Rob was still feeling weak and he loathed being in such a state. His father had taken some cattle to market. He hated seeing them go, so was always sad on market days, and though he said over and over again, "We have to live,"it did not make him feel better. Worse still, a letter telling his father to appear in Court in three week's time had dropped through the letter-box just before he had left and had dampened his spirits still further.

At eleven o'clock Sarah arrived with her mother. "I've brought the dressage markers. Is that all right?"

she asked, bursting into the kitchen. The markers were oil drums painted white with letters on them in black; "I'll ride over on Spangles and show you what we're going to do later," she said, smiling her father's smile, while her mother added, "Are you sure you don't mind Mrs Bartrum? Please say if you would rather Sarah didn't come over."

But Rob's mother said that it was a pleasure to see Sarah and that she was always more than welcome. "Rob doesn't see other children of his own age," she continued, "and he needs help with his riding."

Spangles was a new pony, a liver chestnut with a white streak down his face and unusual flaxen tail and mane. He was quick and bouncy and not very good at dressage. Later that day Rob held Spangles while Sarah marked out the arena and his mother put Snowman in his stable. Then Rob sat on a chair and observed Sarah riding a test. And now he ached to be riding again.

He learned about an extended trot; about a sitting trot; about turns on the haunches. He learned about changing the rein, and leading off on either leg and on how to ride a circle. Spangles rushed everything, and when Sarah halted to salute before riding out of the arena on a loose rein, he chewed his bit and fretted.

Rob's mother clapped. Sarah said, "It was a rotten test. I overshot every marker and forgot to change my diagonals. And Spangles rushed every movement, but perhaps it gives you an idea of what dressage is like, Rob. I'll bring some long poles over tomorrow and then we can trot over poles on the ground, and put them on the dressage markers and have a few jumps when you feel like it Rob."

"Not yet. He's not ready to jump yet," cried Melanie Bartrum. "Why tomorrow will be the first time he's used his saddle and bridle."

Rob thought then what a long way he had to go to catch up with Sarah and was disheartened.

"Shall I come over tomorrow then?" asked Sarah smiling.

And Rob said, "Yes", though he would rather have spent a day or two riding without her. And his mother smiled and said, "That will be lovely Sarah. Thank you for everything."

Sarah rode away while Rob and his mother turned Snowman into the paddock again and went indoors and Rob asked, "Will I ever ride as well as Sarah, Mum?"

"Yes of course you will. It may take a little time though," she replied. But her words did not comfort Rob, because he knew she was always hopeful and encouraging even if it meant lying.

Later Rob's father returned half drunk from market. He sat in a chair in the kitchen saying, "They were all sold. I just hope they aren't being shipped abroad. One never knows where they go nowadays." Then he added, "By the way, I've heard some disturbing news. I'm not sure whether it's good or bad—Bill's dead."

"Dead?" shouted Rob. "Really dead."

"So I've heard. The police went up to get a further statement from him and found him dead outside his caravan. He had a bottle of whisky in his hand. It'll be in the evening paper."

There was a long silence before Rob said, "Snowman's safe then?"

"As long as his little girl doesn't turn up. Apparently he had a child some years ago; but I'm told she married an American and went abroad," replied Rob's father while his mother said, "I think this calls for a celebration. Didn't I tell you we were out of the wood, Rob?"

And Rob didn't touch wood this time because he was so busy thinking that one day someone might decide to claim the caravan and the rough patch of land where Snowman had stood tethered for so many weeks. And whoever it was might claim Snowman too. Rob got up and went outside and told Snowman that Bill was dead and the old pony nuzzled his hair and blew down his neck and seemed to understand.

Later Rob put the new saddle and bridle on to Snowman and rode him round the paddock. He knew how to hold the reins and how to sit with his heels down, with plenty of room behind him in the saddle. But his left leg was awkward and the reins felt stiff in his fingers and he didn't feel as close to Snowman as he had riding bareback. He steered the old pony between the oil drums, and tried a sitting trot. He rode into the centre and halting at X, took his hat off to imaginary judges. None of it was as hard as he had expected, and now he was filled with hope for in spite of his fall, he could still ride and Bill was dead.

Sarah was a good instructor. She wouldn't let Rob school for too long. "Twenty minutes is quite enough to begin with and if you keep riding the same test

Snowman will learn it and then he'll be ahead of you, and judges hate that," she said.

In three days Rob improved tremendously. Sarah called him a natural. His mother was thrilled.

When the local paper arrived on Friday, there was a photograph of Bill inside it. Alongside was written, LOCAL CHARACTER FOUND DEAD NEAR CARAVAN. It described Bill as a pedlar, who had died with a whisky bottle in his hand; a man of seventy years who had married a local girl of eighteen, who had lived with her for a short time in a Council house. Rob's mother read it slowly. "Seventy! I thought he was eighty at least. There won't be many at his funeral," she exclaimed.

"You never know. A whole crowd of pedlars could turn up," said Rob's father. "They could play gipsy music!"

Rob said that he was glad that Bill was dead because now they could forget he ever existed, and enjoy Snowman. Sarah said the same thing. "We can stop worrying now and get on with our riding," she said.

Soon Rob was trotting over poles on the ground; then over small jumps. Snowman seemed to know what to do. "Once upon a time he was really schooled by someone, any fool can see that," Sarah said. Soon he was going better than Spangles who still hated standing still. They put the poles higher on the oil drums. They made doubles and triples and parallel bars. Snowman jumped everything with a flourish, and a shake of his old grey head.

"He must have won prizes in the past, hundreds of

them, said Sarah enviously. "And he's so wise and patient; it's incredible."

They found hardboard and made a wall. They lugged an old gate from the top field where it had lain for years and repaired it. Rob had not seen Arif for weeks now, but he did not miss him. He was far too busy riding to miss anyone. As the evenings lengthened, Sarah and Rob rode down the bridleways and byways. Rob grew fatter and fitter. Often now he forgot his limp altogether.

Melanie Bartrum was proved right, for few people attended Bill's funeral. In all the years he had been there, he had done nothing for the village. So only the Publican from the Gooseberry Bush was there and a couple of friends, old men with rough hands and bent backs who spoke an ancient dialect which hardly anyone could understand. Sarah tolled the church bell for Bill. "It was so sad," she said afterwards. "All those years he lived here, yet there wasn't a single bunch of flowers on his grave."

"He got what he deserved," replied Rob.

They were sitting in the tack room cleaning Snowman's tack. Sarah had brought a horse show schedule with her. "There's three classes for you Rob—jumping under 13.2, 12 and under; jumping with dressage; and pair jumping, if you don't mind pairing with me and Spangles."

"Great, terrific," Rob said.

"It will be your debut. You will probably do better than me," Sarah said. "Spangles is so flighty and you know how he hates walls."

Rob's parents were filled with pride when they

saw him jumping. His mother called it a miracle. His father said that Rob was a chip off the old block, but which block, wondered Sarah? Pippa grew old. Spring turned into summer. Rob had never been as he was now. He woke every morning with joy in his heart. He was always outside now building jumps or grooming Snowman. His school work improved. He became more handsome and grew taller. The grass inside Bill's electric fence grew high and lank. Birds nested in the eaves of the caravan. The shed where Snowman had once lived collapsed. Slowly nature and the wild animals took over; the caravan filled with mice. Rabbits burrowed beneath it, ragwort bloomed yellow amid the dank grass. Creepers wound themselves round the little fencing dragging it down.

The Publican gave away the stool Bill had sat on so often in a corner of The Gooseberry Bush. Soon people stopped talking about Bill; they had other things on their minds. His grave remained untended; no-one offered to pay for a gravestone. School broke up. Snowman was looking as good as he would ever look now. His coat gleamed white, his eyes shone, his hoofs were neat and shod. Rob's fall and stay in hospital seemed little more than a bad dream. Melanie Bartrum went back to working at the Home for the Elderly. Charlie Bartrum decided to apply to the Council for a holiday camping and caravan site. "There's no money in farming these days," he said. The electric fence disappeared beneath the onslaught of weeds and creepers. The ragwort grew ever higher. Baby rabbits played around the caravan.

Rob and Sarah made plans for the Show. Spangles

was living at the farm now. Rob's parents would do anything for Sarah. In their eyes she was beyond criticism. She had broken with Jane, just as Rob had broken with Arif. "She was so boring," said Sarah alluding to Jane. "She was always bothering over things like hair slides and make up."

"Arif only thinks about money. It's money, money all day long. But will he be happy when he has it?" asked Rob.

"I expect so. People like that usually are. Dad believes money is the root of all evil, but I'm not so sure, because if you have enough, you can save horses from being slaughtered and rescue ill-treated dogs and cats," Sarah said.

"We need it. We need it all the time," said Rob. "Soon I'll have to get a job because I can't keep asking Mum for entry fees."

"My aunt thinks we could horse deal. She'd buy the ponies and we would school them on and sell them at a profit. What do you think?"

"Think?" cried Rob. "I think it's great. But are we good enough?"

"Well not yet, but soon," said Sarah laughing. "Your Dad can build a cross country course and charge people for using it. We can take liveries."

"But who will do the mucking out?"

"I will."

Afterwards Rob would look back at this time as one of the happiest in his life. The sun seemed to be forever shining, the flowers always in full bloom. Pippa grew blind, but he did not notice it. Rob's mother grew weary, but he did not see that either.

His father went to Court and was fined an undisclosed sum for obstructing the police, and he hardly cared. That's how it was—his shortened leg, his limp, his self consciousness caused by them, all suddenly took a back seat in Rob's life. Snowman was fit and he could ride; by comparison little else mattered.

Chapter Ten

THE SHOW

The night before the Show, Sarah and Rob cleaned their tack polishing every buckle until it shone like polished glass. They groomed their ponies, bandaged their tails. They washed Spangles' white socks and most of Snowman. They cleaned their riding boots, brushed their coats, steamed their riding hats. The forecast was good. Their parents were bringing picnic lunches to the Show. Sarah decided to plait Spangles because he was entered for The Family Pony Class. "We won't win anything of course; it's just for fun," she said almost bubbling over with excitement.

"I don't expect to win anything either," replied Rob. "I just want to be there."

Rob read the Dressage Test before he went to sleep that night. Outside there was a moon and a cow was lowing. It was like any other night, but special, because tomorrow was the Show, and he had never ridden in public before. He could hear his parents talking downstairs and Pippa snoring in the passage outside his door. He thought back and saw himself before Snowman came to live at Yew Tree Farm, and Sarah became his friend. What a wimp he had been then! Happiness and excitement ran through him now like sudden sunlight on a winter day. Tomorrow was something he had never expected, never dreamed of; he would no longer be just the Bartrum boy with the crippled leg. Tomorrow he would show the world, that he was as good as anyone else. Tomorrow would be like a new beginning.

"Halt at X, salute the judges, ride out on a loose rein," he muttered. He knew the test, each movement was etched on his mind. He knew the difference between an ordinary and an extended trot, he knew when to change legs and how to halt Snowman smoothly and effortlessly. He had learnt it all. Rob went through the test once more in his mind before falling asleep to dream that he was cantering Snowman on and on towards a tree which never grew any nearer. In his sleep he muttered, "Why does it keep moving Mum?" And she replied, "Because it wants to."

Rob woke early, but not as early as Sarah who, when he looked out of his bedroom window, was already in the paddock catching the ponies. His father was seeing to the animals. His mother had let out the hens. There was a whispering breeze, but in spite of it the day was growing hotter every moment.

The ponies were still clean. Sarah plaited Spangles sighing over dropped needles. Rob strapped both ponies with the body brush; then polished them with the stable rubber Sarah had brought with her. He oiled their hoofs and felt sick inside when he thought of what lay ahead, because he wanted to do well more than anything else at that moment. He and Sarah ate breakfast in the kitchen while the ponies ate small feeds, and Melanie put a picnic and collapsible chairs in the car; then coats for fear it would rain, and her own boots for the same reason. Gobbling breakfast cereal, Sarah and Rob went through the dressage test once more. Rob felt as though he had been waiting for this day for ever.

"All I want is one rosette, just one," he said as they tacked up the ponies, mounted, rode into the sunshine.

"You'll win something. I know you will, Rob," Sarah said.

The ponies knew they were going somewhere exciting and important. They knew it by the bandages still on their tails, by the extra grooming and the plaits on Spangles' flaxen mane. They tossed their heads and hurried. Sarah talked about Spangles. "Dad is buying him for me week by week," she said.

"I thought your aunt was rich. Why doesn't she give you Spangles?" Rob asked.

"Because rich people are often like that, that's why they're rich," replied Sarah laughing.

"What's happened to Squirrel?" asked Rob.

"He's winning prizes all over the Midlands. He was too good for me," she said.

And too expensive! thought Rob dispassionately.

"Don't you see Jane any more?" he asked.

"No. She was nasty about you, if you really want to know," replied Sarah laughing. "What about Arif?"

"He grew tired of hearing about Snowman, and he never did like Pippa," replied Rob.

"Jane was always cadging something," continued Sarah. "And she was awful about you in hospital. I mean she didn't have to eat half the chocolates we brought you, did she?"

"It didn't matter. I didn't mind." Rob felt nearer to Sarah now than he had felt to anyone other than his parents. And the ponies liked each other, though each was trying to outwalk the other.

Soon they could see the Showground in the distance. Rob felt weak in his stomach. He had never appeared in public before, never competed at anything. His leg had seen to that, for it had always seemed to be there saying, 'No. don't.' People will see me and say, 'poor unlucky boy.' They'll say, 'look he's crippled.' But he knew that no-one noticed. Horseboxes passed them now.

"I feel quite sick with excitement. I always do. How about you?" asked Sarah.

"The same," Rob answered. "I feel as though I'm about to get stitch."

"Mum calls it butterflies in your stomach. Dad says it doesn't matter whether one wins or not; it is totally unimportant," Sarah said as the man at the gate waved them on into the Showground.

"The Clear Round Jumping starts in ten minutes," said Sarah consulting her watch. "I suggest we go straight there and warm our ponies up for Jumping with Dressage."

I never imagined myself doing this, thought Rob, not in my wildest dreams.

They each paid a pound to go in the Clear Round Jumping. Spangles hit the gate. Rob took the wrong course, so neither won a rosette. But the way Snowman jumped put Rob at ease; for he seemed to know exactly what to do. It was Rob who was making the mistakes. Their parents arrived. Rob's father had brought a camera he had never used before. His mother plied them with lemon squash and ginger-bread, but they weren't hungry nor thirsty. Sarah fetched their numbers from the Secretary's tent. Her mother patted the ponies. Jim, the farm vet, came across to join them. "How's my patient then? It looks like a complete recovery. Well done," he said.

More and more horseboxes arrived, more and more riders. "You're number 42, don't forget Rob," said Sarah tying his number to his back. His father hoped it would be lucky. His mother gave Snowman a carrot.

"There's plenty here by the look of it," his father said.

"There always is," replied Sarah.

They were called to the Collecting Ring. A girl on a bay was riding the Dressage Test.

"I feel sick," said Sarah.

"Same here," agreed Rob.

The girl was wearing a dark navy coat. Her pony was part Arab. They moved altogether perfectly and completed the test without faltering.

"We haven't a hope," said Sarah.

"It doesn't matter," replied Rob. "It's enough to be here."

"There will be the jumping too," said Sarah. "One fence down can make a heck of a difference."

"They're calling you now. Good luck," Rob said.

Spangles champed his bit and hurried. Sarah sat very straight in the saddle, too straight, thought

Rob. But her sitting trot was perfect and so was her turn on the haunches. Rob did not see the rest for now he was warming Snowman up, walking and trotting round the Collecting Ring, ready to go in.

"It was terrible," called Sarah riding out. He rushed everything. Rob could see that she was close to tears. The Collecting Ring Stewards called him into the ring and he rode round outside the dressage arena until the judge at the far end tooted her car horn. Snowman hurried in. He knew what to do. He always seemed to know. Rob took off his hat and saluted the judge sitting in her car at the end of the arena. He felt quite calm now, relieved to be there at last.

Snowman broke into a canter in the extended trot. Otherwise he was completely accurate, as accurate as clockwork. There was a burst of clapping as Rob rode out.

"Well done Rob, well done!" cried his mother.

He wished she would be quiet, but loved her too much to tell her so.

"That was terrific," she cried, throwing her arms around Snowman's neck. "Oh he's such a poppet."

"Well done son," his father said.

Rob turned to Sarah. "What do you think?" he asked.

"Better than mine, a bit wooden, but marvellous for a first time," she said.

"Well you can't expect to do everything right the first time," his mother said defensively.

"I know that," Rob said. "I don't expect to win anything Mum. Of course I don't."

106

"You have to accept you're only a beginner," his father suggested, while his mother cried, "I still think it was a fantastic performance."

They waited for their marks to be pinned up and saw that they were neither good not bad, just somewhere in the middle. They mounted and rode across to the jumping ring. Rob looked at the fences there and his mouth felt dry—they were higher than he had ever jumped before. Snowman looked, then shook his old grey head knowingly.

"Spangles will never jump the wall. It's too big," Sarah said, while Rob's mother said, "Are you sure you can do them love?"

"Of course I can," replied Rob.

"That's right son, you go in and show them," his father said. "Show them what you're made of, that you're not a Bartrum for nothing."

Rob rode away. He rode through the horseboxes, past thoroughbreds and Arabs and tiny Shetlands. He rode past a Rolls Royce and three Range Rovers and several horseboxes and suddenly he knew how poor the Bartrums were. But it doesn't matter he thought, because I don't want what they've got. I just want home and Snowman. And then he saw Sarah riding towards him in tears.

"Spangles stopped three times at the wall. And they're calling your number," she said.

"I'm sorry," Rob called and cantered across the Showground.

"Oh there you are," said the Collecting Ring Steward. "You can go straight in."

Rob had looked at the course, now he looked again,

as he had seen professionals do, waiting for the bell. And he wasn't scared at all, just filled with a sense of awe that he was there at all. Then the bell went and Snowman pricked his ears and went into a wonderfully smooth canter, as though jumping was something he had done all his life. And he felt so calm and cool that Rob felt no nerves at all as he went with him sitting still and quiet, giving him his head as he came into each fence, looking like a natural as Sarah was to say afterwards.

The fences came and went, brush, wall, rails, combination, stile, parallel bars, upright and finally a spread which Snowman took fast, giving a small triumphant buck afterwards. Rob had lost control by this time, but Snowman took him through the exit at a gallop.

As he stopped, Rob heard a burly man ask, "Isn't that Charlie Bratrum's crippled boy? Well, he looks all right today, doesn't he?" And then Rob was surrounded by smiling congratulatory faces. Snowman was smothered in pats while the loudspeaker announced, "Number 42 had a clear round."

"There are only three other clears so far, so you must get a rosette, Rob," cried Sarah.

"I never knew he could do it," beamed Charlie Bartrum.

Even Jim the vet now appeared to congratulate Rob. "He was worth saving then," he said smiling, looking at Snowman in wonder. "And he knows his job too."

"He took me round. I didn't have to do a thing," said Rob.

"He must be worth a fortune, even at his age," said Jim Hubbard. His words made Rob suddenly afraid. Then he smiled again—Bill's little girl didn't exist, didn't they all know that? And if by any chance she did exist she was far away in the US.

Rob dismounted and loosened Snowman's girths, as a large woman approached in jeans and a turtle necked shirt and asked, "Will he be for sale? He's just what I'm looking for for my daughter here. He looks as safe as houses and a real school master," she said.

Rob shook his head. "No, he'll never be sold. He's fifteen years old," he said, as though that settled the matter.

"I don't mind his age. I want something safe which will cart my little girl round the Shows. I'm willing to pay a lot, anything you ask," the woman said.

Rob looked at the girl standing beside her mother, dressed up in riding clothes, as smart as a model in a shop window. She had red bows in her hair and a small scowly face. "I want him Mummy. I want him now," she cried.

"I know darling. We'll talk to Daddy. He'll know what to do," her mother said striding away while Rob muttered, "He's not for sale," while fear seemed to grow inside him, snaking through his body like poison.

"They're calling you in for the jump off. Wake up Rob," Sarah called. "Hurry up. They're drawing lots to decide who goes first."

Rob pulled up his girths and mounted. There were six clear rounds and he was to go third.

"Watch the others. See how to cut corners. They

haven't put the fences up, so you should be all right," Sarah said.

"You don't have to jump the stile and the gate," his mother added, putting on dark glasses.

"A woman wanted to buy Snowman for her nasty little girl," Rob said.

"Well we can't sell him can we?" replied his mother.

"I'm scared just the same," said Rob.

"Don't be ridiculous. Watch the other competitors," Sarah told him, pulling up the girths another notch. "You can cut inside the stile. Cut all the corners you can. Ride as though your life depends on it."

Snowman cantered into the ring, cantered a circle and waited for the bell, his old ears pricked. Another second and they were off. Rob rode fast, faster than he had ever ridden before. Snowman knew what he was doing. He lengthened his stride and flew. Rob could hear someone shouting, "Go on Rob. You show them," and knew it was his father, wild with excitement, twisting his cap in his hands.

Then it was over. Sarah had timed it. "You're three seconds too slow. But you're still in the running," she said.

Rob dismounted on to his good leg. He did not care as much as his parents, he saw that now. Proving that he could ride mattered more to him than prizes. In the end he was third and soon he rode into the ring with the other winners and lined up to loud applause. Snowman tossed his head. He knew he was among the winners. Then they all cantered round the ring and out into the Showground.

"Not bad for a beginner," Rob's father said. "Well done." His camera whirred. "One for the album," he said patting Snowman.

Then Rob thought, I wish Sarah had won, because without her I wouldn't be here. He remembered asking his mother, "Will I ever ride as well as she does?" and it had seemed impossible; now he had proved otherwise, but of course thanks were due to Sarah and to Snowman, for if he had refused or stopped suddenly, Rob knew that he would have gone straight on over his head.

Sarah appeared now bearing his test sheet. The judge wrote that Snowman was stiff. "She doesn't mention your leg position so someone must have told her about your wonky leg. You're ninth overall. I'm fourth in the dressage," she said. "So you'll only have a rosette for the jumping."

"Great," Rob said.

It was then that another woman appeared. She was small with long hair, tight jeans, loafers, and a T-shirt with a horse on it.

"It's Snowy, dear old Snowy. I'd know him anywhere," she cried. "And you're Rob." In panic Rob stared at her and saw Bill in her face for her ears were set back in the same way as his had been, and she had the same blue eyes. She started to pat Snowman, to pull his ears. "Do you remember me, your old mistress? Do you?" she asked, while Rob's world seemed to be collapsing around him.

"You're Bill's little girl, arn't you?" he asked at last.

"That's right. I know where you live. I'm just over from the USA. See you Rob," she said. "I'm coming to see you later."

Rob wanted to find his parents now, to tell them, to tell Sarah—anyone, just to say, "Bill's little girl does exist and she's here." But now he was being called to a collecting ring to compete in the Novice Jumping.

Chapter Eleven

WAITING

The rest of the Show would always be a blur to Rob. He fell off in the Novice Jumping. Snowman went too fast for him and Rob's heart wasn't in it any more. It was somewhere else watching Snowman leaving. The two women's words kept echoing in his head . . . " I'll pay anything you ask," and, "yes I'm coming to see you later." They hung over him till his mind was frantic with frightening possibilities.

He told Sarah. "It may be all right. She may be okay. Americans are very generous, we all know that," Sarah replied.

"But she's Bill's daughter. And what about the other woman?

Supposing they get together. They may even know each other. Can't you see what's going to happen?" demanded Rob, his voice wracked with anxiety.

"No I can't. Why do you always look on the black side Rob? It's so depressing," replied Sarah.

Snowman went too fast in the pair jumping and knocked down the gate. Sarah said that it had been a disgraceful performance. "You didn't even try," she shouted furiously. "You know Snowman can't jump fast. So why didn't you slow up?"

Rob didn't answer. He dropped the potatoes in the

Potato Race. Snowman knocked down a post in the Bending Race and was eliminated. Rob failed to hear the music stop in the Musical Poles because at that moment he was imagining Bill's daughter leading Snowman into a horsebox. And he fumbled and lost a stirrup in the Flag Race. He could feel Snowman's dismay beneath him, for Snowman liked winning. Rob always knew what the old pony was thinking. He knew that Snowman had been surprised to see Bill's daughter but not overjoyed. Rob thought that maybe he was trying harder than usual, because he didn't want to be taken away from probably, the best home he had ever known.

Spangles was bedecked with rosettes by this time. Sarah was beaming. Rob's parents had gone home before Rob had been able to tell them about Bill's daughter. Now he was afraid that they would strike some sort of deal with her without him. He wanted to leave straightaway, but Sarah insisted on staying until the last points were counted in the gymkhana championship, and as she was reserve champion it paid off. Rob was relieved when they left the show at last. He wanted to hurry but Sarah said they had to think of the ponies who had had a long day. She didn't say that she would have dismounted and led Spangles if it hadn't been for Rob's leg.

As they rode onto the road, she said, "Do cheer up Rob. We've had a lovely day and I'm sure everything's going to be all right." Because she was happy, she wanted Rob to be happy. "You're making a mountain out of a molehill. It's so stupid," she said.

Rob wouldn't talk and couldn't be happy, until he

114

knew that Snowman would be staying at Yew Tree Farm. The success he had enjoyed at the Show only made a parting seem worse.

"I know what will happen—that woman with her simpering tot will buy him. I feel it in my bones. She'll offer two thousand pounds for him. I know she will. She was mad to have him. Then she'll cart him round the Shows, Show after Show, just so that her nasty little brat can be successful. She won't care about Snowman."

"I'm not listening to you," retorted Sarah trotting ahead. It was six o'clock now. Soon every piece of road, every tree was familiar for they were nearly home.

"I feel as though I am going to the gallows," cried Rob in anguish as they saw Yew Tree Farm snug in the valley.

Sarah didn't answer. She was used to her aunt selling the ponies she rode; that's why her parents were buying Spangles on what her father called the 'never, never'.

"And by the way," she said as they turned into the farmyard, "No-one noticed your beastly leg, not even the judges so you can stop feeling sorry for yourself, just for five minutes."

"I'm not sorry for myself. I'm sorry for Snowman," replied Rob throwing himself to the ground, his eyes suddenly blinded with tears.

His father had mucked out the stable. There was food and water waiting for both the ponies. His mother rushed from the hen house clutching a basket of eggs. "So you're back. How did you do? You must take some eggs home with you Sarah. How many would you like?" she said.

"I saw Bill's little girl. She was there. She called Snowman Snowy. She's not in America. She's here," said Rob glumly.

"Oh no! What did she say?"

"She's coming here later. I thought she might be here already. What are we going to do Mum?"

"Did she say she wanted him back?"

"Not exactly. But there was another woman who wanted him. She's willing to pay anything we ask," Rob replied.

"I know, you told me. But don't be too downhearted Rob. And just look at Sarah's rosettes. You really had a field day. Well done. Come in both of you and have something to eat and I bet you're thirsty. I've just made a fresh batch of gingerbread."

They found Rob's father making tea. "I'm proud of you Rob, I really am. Our ugly duckling of a pony really has turned into a swan. Jim couldn't believe his eyes. He thought you must have been feeding him cannabis or something sinister. He said he had never seen such a transformation," said Charlie Bartrum happily.

"It's because the pony is happy here," said Rob's mother passing round the gingerbread.

Presently after Sarah had undone Spangles' plaits they turned the ponies into the paddock and watched them roll over and over in the grass.

"I have to go," Sarah said. "But ring me later, Rob and tell me what happens. I'm sorry I was cross, but I hated such a lovely day being spoilt. I do care about Snowman—desperately." She mounted her bike and rode away. And everything was very quiet now in the farmyard. The hens were going to their hen house for the night. The cats were looking for mice. The birds had stopped singing. The other animals were eating, and the sun was moving to the West.

This has been the best summer of my life. Snowman is the best pony there's ever been, and I'll never forget that, thought Rob. Whatever happens I'll never forget it; I'll always remember.

Pippa appeared and stood in front of him with faded old eyes and a slow wag of her tail. He knew what she was saying. She was saying, "Why are you out here all alone? Why don't you come inside?" Snowman raised his head and nickered to him, softly, a private message of devotion. Rob's shorter leg started to ache. It had been a long day.

He went inside. "What are we going to do?" he asked.

"If she wants Snowman, she'll have to pay for all the time he's been here," his father replied.

"Perhaps you should get the whisky out; it might soften her up a bit," his mother said. "After all it worked wonders with Bill."

They sat and waited. "I feel as though I'm sitting by a death bed," said Rob's mother presently. "I'd better get the supper."

"I don't want any supper. Why is she so long?" Rob asked.

"Perhaps she's down at the pub," suggested his father.

"I don't like her. She called me honey," he said unreasonably.

"She may be quite pleasant," suggested his mother.

"But she's Bill's daughter," answered Rob's father.

"But she may be like her mother," retorted Melanie Bartrum.

Rob wanted to cry, but remained dry-eyed. Tears would have been a relief. Then the telephone rang. Rob seized the receiver, his heart leaping inside him. But it was only Sarah asking, "Has she been yet?"

"No," Rob said gloomily, because somehow he had hoped the call would be good news.

"I'm sorry," Sarah said and put down the receiver.

"She hasn't been yet," Sarah told her mother.

"And it's your bedtime darling."

"I don't care. I can't go to bed until I know what's happening to Snowman," replied Sarah.

"Perhaps the woman's gone back to the USA. Perhaps she's forgotten she ever arranged to go to Yew Tree Farm. Perhaps she's that sort of person," Sarah's mother said.

Her father was writing tomorrow's sermon. After a time Sarah went to bed, but she couldn't sleep.

"She's not coming," said Rob's mother clearing away the supper things. "You look exhausted Rob. Go to bed, we'll wake you if she calls. I promise." It was nearly midnight. Rob dragged himself up the stairs to bed. He ached all over. It seemed to have been the longest day of his life.

"Damn the woman for putting us through this," said Charlie Bartrum downing a whisky.

"I'd like to kill her," replied Melanie Bartrum.

"What do you expect—she's Bill's daughter," said Charlie Bartrum bitterly.

"She's not the first person to let us down, is she? Perhaps she'll be here in the morning." Melanie Bartrum was suddenly tired beyond words. The triumph at the Show was soured. She too would have liked to weep. Instead she let Pippa out for a last time, locked the doors, said "Come to bed Charlie. There's no point in staying up. Maybe Rob misunderstood. Maybe she'll never come here."

"She'll be here," replied Charlie Bartrum going upstairs to bed. "She'll be here wanting something you'll see. A leopard doesn't change its spots that easily. How much do you have in your bank account?"

"Not enough, not more than a thousand pounds."

"It should be enough."

"It will leave me with nothing."

"It won't be the first time will it? And we can always sell something. What about your dressing table, it's an antique," suggested Charlie Bartrum.

"It was my mother's."

"Never mind."

Rob heard them talking and wished he didn't love Snowman so much. Somewhere far away a clock struck one.

The next morning they overslept. Rob woke first wondering, what's wrong. Why am I so unhappy? Then he remembered. He drew back his curtains and looked out. The ponies were besieged by flies at the paddock gate—Snowman was still there! He rushed out in his pyjamas and put Snowman in his stable and Spangles in the building next door which had once been a food store. The sun was up. All the animals were waiting to be fed. The cats purred round his ankles. Pippa whined. The hens clustered round him with their chicks while others threw themselves against a hen house door. The old tractor stood silent waiting to spring into life; everything was waiting for Charlie Bartrum to appear, the boss, the governor, their God.

Rob took tea to his parents in bed who were horrified by the lateness of the hour. "Whatever possessed us to sleep so long?" cried his mother, while his father gulped the tea out of politeness, undoing the buttons of his pyjamas with his other hand.

"No sign of her then?" he asked.

"Not yet. But there's still time," Rob said.

"Either she'll call or she won't. It's as simple as that. And there's not a thing we can do about it," said his father.

They all jumped when there was a knock on the back door. But it was only Sarah flustered and straight out of bed, calling, "Any news? Did she call?"

Half pleased, half disappointed because it wasn't Bill's daughter, Rob shook his head. "Not a sign," he said.

"Perhaps we should go to the caravan. Perhaps she's there," suggested Sarah. "Come on, let's run."

Rob was dressed by this time. He put on trainers. The dew was drying on the grass. "If she calls don't discuss anything till I'm back Mum," he shouted. Hearing his voice, Snowman whinnied from the stable.

But of course Rob couldn't run, and Sarah had to wait for him. Humiliated he said, "I'm sorry," while Sarah asked, "Shall I go ahead and look?"

"Yes, all right." He hated being left behind.

On the hill a magpie was eating the remains of a rabbit. There were burrows everywhere. It seemed years since he had brought Snowman home through the snow just before Christmas, yet it wasn't quite nine months ago.

Sarah reached the top of the hill. There was nothing there—the caravan had gone. "All gone," she said running back to Rob. "The caravan's disappeared; there's no sign of anyone."

"Are you sure?"

"Of course I am. I'm not blind for goodness sake," snapped Sarah.

When they reached home again, Rob's mother had breakfast waiting for them in the kitchen. "I don't think she's going to bother us. I think she's gone back to America," she said. "I think everything's going to be all right Rob. Your Dad agrees with me."

"She said she would call on us," replied Rob obstinately. "And I want her to. I want everything settled once and for all, for ever and ever. I want Snowman safe here until he dies. Okay?" Anger had come back into his voice. He wasn't tired any more. He was ready to fight to keep Snowman.

"I can't believe that we were at a Horse Show yesterday. It seems years ago already," Sarah said eating scrambled eggs on toast, while Rob only played with his, leaving most of it on the side of his plate.

And then they all heard a car. It came into the farmyard, a large long-nosed car, with a little woman sitting at the wheel, with dark glasses hiding bright blue eyes—Bill's daughter.

Chapter Twelve

NO MORE HATE

"Sorry about last night honey" she said getting out of the car and smiling at Rob. "I ran into old friends and couldn't escape. But here I am."

Rob's mouth fell open. Fear silenced him.

"Can I go in honey?"

"Yes of course, this way," replied Sarah after a moment leading the way indoors where Rob's parents were waiting standing close together prepared to be accused of taking Snowman unlawfully in spite of the piece of paper Bill had signed; expecting every hand to be against them, as it had been at the siege.

"What a cute house. Can I sit down?" Rob's mother pulled out a chair for her. "Let's all sit down?" she said coming back to life. "Would you like some tea, or coffee? Or something stronger?"

"A spot of whisky, real Scotch," offered Rob's father.

"Thank you no, a cup of real English tea will be great," she said. "Let me introduce myself. I'm Jenny Forbes, Bill's daughter."

"Glad to meet you Jenny," said Rob's mother holding out her hand. His father shook hands with her too. It's like a business meeting, Rob thought glumly. Mum's going to offer all her savings to buy Snowman. It isn't fair. We saved his life. If it wasn't for us he would be dead. He stared at Jenny Forbes, blue eyes gazing into his.

"We saved your pony's life," he said.

"I know. I know the whole story. I came to say thank you honey. That's why I'm here. I haven't come to take Snowy away. I've come to pay my dues, okay. I owe you everything. I don't care about my father. He was a horrible dirty old man. Snowy, sorry honey, Snowman was the only thing I cared about for years and years. There wasn't anyone else honey. He was my whole existence."

"And you schooled him and taught him to jump?" asked Rob slowly.

"Yeah, with a bit of help from the Pony Club, not the one here, another one. I had to win, you see honey, I had nothing else. Poor old Snowy, what I put him through. I feel guilty now. I rode him almost to death sometimes. I was a hateful kid, honey, but I hadn't anything else."

Rob was starting to understand. "The poor pony was tethered in our council house garden till the neighbours started to complain. Then my Dad found him a patch of land somewhere and that's where he lived, summer and winter. It was real tough for him," she said. "I rode him after school. I rode him in the dark, and in the early morning. No-one liked me. They called my father a pedlar and a tramp, which, let's face it, he was, but as long as I was on Snowy I was all right, everyone's equal. Do you get me, honey."

Rob nodded. He knew the feeling. For hadn't it

124

been the same for him with his disability? Wasn't he, sitting on Snowman suddenly equal too?

"And I wouldn't dream of taking him away from you. I simply want to reward you for what you've done, you and your parents. I've only got dollars, but you can cash them at the bank, no problem —a thousand each, is that all right, a thousand to you Rob and the rest to your parents. Okay honey?"

Rob had turned red. He didn't know what to say. He had hated Bill's little girl so much, inside himself, for so long. And he had been wrong all the time. Now he could only feel guilty.

"Come on, don't be shy honey," she held out a fistful of dollars to him. Her hands were smaller than Bill's and she wore a wedding ring.

"We don't want money, love. Keeping Snowman is quite enough," replied his mother sharply.

"We're all right for money. We're glad we did what we did and we only want bygones to be bygones. You can't help your father being how he was," his mother continued.

"Listen, two thousand dollars is peanuts to me. I've got my own salon in the States. I may not look like it now, but I'm quite well off. And I want Snowman to be happy; I know he will be here. This is the last thing I can do for an old friend, because he thought I would return to him one day if he had my pony. But I let old Snowy down, I never went back. And it's been on my conscience ever since. So do me a favour will you, honey. Take the money and let's be friends."

125

Sarah looked at Rob and said, "Go on, take it. You know you need it."

Rob looked at the money. "Well I do need a rug for Snowman, a warm winter one and things like hoof oil and a body brush," he said slowly.

"So you'll take it," said Jenny and pushed it into his hands.

She left the other dollars on the table and said, "Now I am writing a letter giving you Snowman, so that there will be no more sieges. You see, I've learnt the whole story," she added laughing. She wrote on a piece of paper the following: *I, Jennifer Forbes, nee Harris, give my old pony Snowy to Robert Bartrum to love and to cherish and when he is old to put him down humanely at home.* Then she dated it and wrote *JC Forbes* at the bottom. Then she handed the piece of paper to Rob saying, "I know he'll be all right with you Rob". And Rob found his eyes were full of tears while he muttered, "Thank you, I'll look after him, I promise."

"Put the piece of paper away safely, because I don't expect to be back in England for years, if ever," said Jenny standing up. "And now for a last farewell to my old pony, and then to see the Rector about a gravestone for my horrible old Dad."

"What about your Mum?" asked Melanie Bartrum.

"She's still alive. She lives nearby in the States," replied Jenny whom Rob would always think of as Bill's little girl. They went outside. Snowman was looking over his stable door. He whinnied when he saw Rob—he always did. But he was not afraid of Jennifer Forbes, just indifferent. She patted his neck and said, "Farewell old friend. You won't miss me, and I don't blame you for it. I wasn't much of a mistress to you.

Then she turned to Rob saying, "And don't sell him however much you're offered. There are quite a few people who have approached me already wanting to buy."

"He'll never be for sale; he's my best friend and you don't sell friends," replied Rob firmly.

Then Jenny handed Rob's mother a card with her name and address on it. "If you're ever in the States give me a buzz and you too, Sarah. Don't forget now," she said.

"She's great. One of the nicest people I've ever met," Sarah said as she drove away. "And she's had such an awful life here," said Rob slowly.

"Occasionally a rotten childhood works that way, not often though. More often the child turns violent," Rob's mother told them walking towards the house. "I do wish people had helped her years ago when she was just a kid."

"School's like that—once you're picked on, you've had it," Rob said. "There's no hope. You're simply bottom of the heap."

"Not all schools," argued Sarah.

"But Snowman's the hero. He taught me how to ride with a bit of help from you," Rob said smiling at Sarah. "And look at what he did for Jennifer!"

"And she called him Snowy and you called him Snowman."

"What a coincidence," laughed Sarah.

"And I don't hate her any more. I don't even hate

Bill. It's rather a sad story, isn't it? He must have loved his daughter so much," Rob said.

"Perhaps now you'll be happy," replied his mother. "Because Snowman really is safe with us now. No-one can take him away."

"And I must do some work," said Charlie Bartrum. "There's no rest for the wicked."

"And I must go home," announced Sarah. "I'm so happy I could cry."

Sarah went home. Her mother met her in the hall. "Guess what darling, Bill's daughter has given a thousand pounds to the Church. Isn't it wonderful? Aren't you surprised?" she asked.

"Not really. You see, I've met her and she's a lovely person. And she's given Snowman to Rob for ever and ever. She was the person who schooled him. She says if we're ever in the States we must visit her."

"So the gloom has lifted at last," her mother said. "Come on, the table needs laying for lunch."

Rob dug up a carrot growing in the vegetable garden and gave it to Snowman. "You're here for ever now," he said. "No-one can take you away ever again," and saying those words seemed to cleanse his whole being.

Without warning the bitterness and hate were gone. Anything is possible he said to himself, one just has to go out for it, to go on and on and never give up. Then he was running indoors shouting, "Oh, I'm so happy." And he had never said it before nor felt as he did now, not once in his whole life.